# MURDER AT MIDNIGHT

DISCARDED

## AVI

SCHOLASTIC PRESS
NEW YORK

# FOR
# MARIANNE
# MEROLA

All rights reserved. Published by Scholastic Press, an imprint of Scholastic Inc., *Publishers since 1920.* SCHOLASTIC, SCHOLASTIC PRESS, and associated logos are trademarks and/or registered trademarks of Scholastic Inc.

LIBRARY OF CONGRESS CATALOGING-IN-PUBLICATION DATA

Avi, 1937–
Murder at midnight / Avi. — 1st ed.    p.    cm.    Summary: Falsely accused of plotting to overthrow King Claudio, scholarly Mangus the magician, along with his street-smart servant boy, Fabrizio, face deadly consequences unless they can track down the real traitor by the stroke of midnight.
ISBN-13: 978-0-545-08090-3
ISBN-10: 0-545-08090-8
[1. Magicians—Fiction. 2. Orphans—Fiction. 3. Renaissance—Italy—Fiction. 4. Mystery and detective stories.] I. Title. PZ7.A953Mu 2009
[Fic]—dc22
2009003214

10 9 8 7 6 5 4 3 2 1        09 10 11 12 13

Printed in the U.S.A.    23
First edition, September 2009

Book design by Marijka Kostiw

# PERGAMONTIO, ITALY
## 1490

# CHAPTER 1

A PALE BEAM OF COLD OCTOBER SUN SLIPPED THROUGH a crack in the old roof and settled on Fabrizio's drowsy eyes. With a flap of his dirty fingers the boy attempted to brush the light away. Failing, he rolled over on his straw mattress and slipped back into a doze. The next moment he sat bolt upright. He had overslept! There were chores to do! Mistress Sophia would soon be leaving to care for her sick sister. And that meant that Master Mangus would be harder to please than ever.

*But it's better than living on the streets,* Fabrizio reminded himself.

During the past year, his parents — ragpickers — had died, leaving him a homeless ten-year-old. Only by relying on his wits and friends did Fabrizio survive the streets of Pergamontio. But a month ago, the City Corporation, which had the responsibility for orphans, bound him over to Mangus the Magician.

It was the magician's wife, Mistress Sophia, who made the arrangements. It was she who insisted that her elderly

3

husband needed a personal servant. She herself proved kind, and Fabrizio was thrilled not to be begging on the streets for a daub of cold, clotted pasta for his dinner. Now he had good food in his belly, a roof over his head, a bed for his back, and even a few coins in his pocket. Besides, not only did Master Mangus have a house with two older servants, there was his amazing magic.

But the old man was *not* happy. He insisted he did *not* need Fabrizio, complaining that the boy was an ignorant, idle chatterer. Mangus was proving a hard master.

Now, with Mistress going away — no one was certain for how long — Fabrizio knew he must be careful not to displease the old man. The last thing he wanted was to go back to the streets.

Fabrizio yanked on his tunic and trousers, tightened his rope belt, drew on his old cloth boots, scurried out of his small attic sleeping space, and all but slid down the rickety ladder. Reaching the second floor, he paused to listen. No one was astir.

Down the steps to the main floor he crept, heading right into his master's study at the rear of the house.

Fabrizio found the room fascinating. A dim and chilly place, the warped oak-beamed ceiling hung low, walls were stained by smoke, and the wooden floor lay as uneven as the sea. It smelled, too, of burnt candles, sealing wax, parchment, bundles of manuscripts, as well as some thirty leather-bound books that lay scattered about.

Two chests of Master Mangus's magic equipment sat in one corner. In another corner stood a reading lectern, a chair in another. Shelves stuffed with books and parchment pages lined the walls. In the room's center was a heavy oak table, laden with more books, more papers. On the table sat a human skull, which Fabrizio always thought was staring at him.

Fabrizio shivered, took up the clay pot that sat on the floor, dumped its cold ashes into a bucket, and refilled it with wood chips and lumps of charcoal. With flint and iron, he sparked the wood until a small fire burned, enough to gentle some warmth into the room.

Using a metal pincer, he plucked up one of the red hot coals and lit the candle that sat inside the skull. The light glowing through its empty sockets had the appearance of living eyes. They reminded him of Mangus, fascinating but angry.

Fabrizio gathered up the books and began to shelve them. It was the third volume — one of Mangus's magic books — that made him pause. Its wondrous pages revealed how to make things change and appear magically. Fabrizio had been studying it secretly.

Setting the book down, he went to the door to see if anyone else had gotten up. All remained still.

Cleaning his fingers with a quick lick of his tongue, Fabrizio placed the book of magic near the skull light and opened it. Unfortunately, he was just beginning to read. Still, there were complex pictures of equipment: boxes, tables, tubes, bowls, all with fascinating diagrams, which, he was sure, revealed ways for a magician to hide, float away, and reappear.

As Fabrizio studied these illustrations, he took some coins — *pezollas* — from his pocket and practiced making them appear and disappear.

Suddenly, he heard the sound of someone coming down the steps. Snapping the book shut, he pocketed the coins, dropped to his knees, and, with a pounding heart, began shoving books onto shelves.

Behind him, the door opened slowly.

"Ah, Fabrizio. Here you are," said a soft voice. Mistress Sophia, a fair, gray-haired woman with a dimpled, kindly face, stepped into the room.

Much relieved, Fabrizio jumped to his feet. "Good morning, Mistress."

"Just a quick word," she said. "The donkey cart taking me to my sister's will be here soon. And Master will be down shortly."

"Yes, Mistress. I'm very sorry you have to go."

Sophia brushed Fabrizio's black hair from his forehead, placed her hands on his narrow shoulders, and gazed earnestly down into his dark eyes.

"Fabrizio, I hope you know how fond of you I've become. Like the child we never had. I do so want you to remain with us. But I fear we've not convinced Master that you need to stay. I know" — she said, preventing him from replying with a finger touch to his lips — "he's been difficult. But while I'm gone, you *must* try extra hard to please him. Take care of him and all his needs. Do your chores well. Find new ones to do. Don't quarrel with the other servants. Work hard at your reading. In short," she said, giving the boy a gentle shake, "think of my being away as your best chance to prove how useful you can be. Make Master Mangus love you as much as I do."

"Yes, Mistress," said Fabrizio earnestly. "It's as someone once told me: No use having the lioness like you if the lion doesn't."

"Exactly right." Sophia laughed and ruffled the boy's hair with affection.

"Mistress, how long will you be gone?"

"It could be a day or a month. My sister isn't far, and she's never as ill as she claims. So much depends on her.

"Now, Fabrizio, listen well: Tonight, Master Mangus is performing his magic at the Sign of the Crown. You've been begging to go. I've urged him to let you take my place at the door collecting money. You'll be pleased to know . . . he's granted my request."

*"Truly?"* cried Fabrizio.

"Your first performance," said Mistress Sophia, smiling at the boy's joy. "But," she added solemnly, "you must do well."

"I will, Mistress!" said Fabrizio, snatching her hand and covering it with kisses. "I promise!"

"Now then," said Sophia. "Get on with your work. And . . . Why not sweep the hallway? When Master comes down, he'll see you working hard at one of my tasks. Remember, you *must* show him how much he needs you."

"Yes, Mistress. I'll make myself as useful as his right hand."

"God keep you," she said, bending down to kiss him on both his cheeks.

"You, too, Mistress," returned Fabrizio, suddenly reaching out and hugging her. "And your sister."

Sophia offered a warm smile and left.

*A performance!* thought Fabrizio as he rushed to shelve the remaining books. Finished, he dashed into the hallway, grabbed a straw broom, and began to sweep vigorously.

Reaching the front door, he unbolted and pulled it

open to brush out the dust. There, on the empty street, stood a man dressed in a monk's black robe. The hood was pulled down so only his eyes were exposed. He was staring at Mangus's house.

"Can I help you, Signore?" Fabrizio called.

"Is this the home of Mangus the Magician?"

"Most wonderfully, yes, Signore."

"Is he performing soon?"

"Tonight, Signore. At the Sign of the Crown. And I," the boy could not resist adding, "shall be there. For the first time!"

The black-robed man drew the hood farther down over his face, turned, and hastened away down the street.

Fabrizio glanced after him and shrugged. The city was full of black robes.

As he hurried back into the house, Fabrizio nearly bumped into Master Mangus coming down the steps.

"Good morning, Master," Fabrizio whispered.

"What's that?" Mangus grunted.

As befit his seventy years of age, Mangus was somewhat stooped. His robe was neat and clean, his carefully cut beard was gray, his hair white, and the folds of his eyes much crinkled. And as far as Fabrizio was concerned, Mangus's pale face suggested the deepest knowledge of things magical and mysterious.

"Good morning, Master," Fabrizio repeated, offering his best smile.

Mangus frowned. "Your mistress will be leaving shortly," he grumbled. "Go fetch her things."

"Yes, Master," said Fabrizio.

He ran up the steps. Halfway up he recalled the black-robed man at their door. *Should I tell Master?*

"Fabrizio!" cried Mangus. "Don't dawdle! You're needed!"

"Yes, Master," said Fabrizio. "Of course, Master." He raced up.

The black robe was forgotten.

# CHAPTER 2

$\mathfrak{T}$HAT NIGHT, IN THE CROWDED BACK ROOM OF THE SIGN of the Crown tavern, Fabrizio was determined to see everything. Since his task — collecting money — would come at the end of Mangus's performance, he had climbed atop an overturned basket behind the audience.

The magician, standing before a yellow backdrop, was costumed in a green velvet robe lined with red silk that peeked out like spots of fire. On his feet were blue Turkish slippers with tips curled like monkey tails. On his head sat a three-peaked hat. From each peak hung a black star.

*Exactly the way a magician should look.* Next moment, Fabrizio scolded himself. *Never mind what he looks like! Watch! Listen! If you want to become a magician, you must learn!*

He stood riveted as Mangus made balls, bones, flowers, and cups appear, disappear, change shape, color, and size. Fabrizio had no doubt that some of what he saw were tricks. He was equally sure the rest was real magic. *How clever of Master to mix the real with tricks!*

A ball was taken from an empty box. *That's a trick,* Fabrizio decided, recalling a diagram from the magic book. A burning candle was pulled from an ear. *That's true magic,* he thought. A box changed into a hat. *True magic, again.* Objects were snatched from noses, sleeves, and elbows. There were flashes of light. Smoke. Real or unreal, everything was wonderful!

"Dear friends!" Mangus said to the enthralled crowd. "Is not the great enterprise of magic to make something from nothing? To make more from less? I believe it is! Therefore, for my final act of magic, I shall do exactly that: create something from nothing. Furthermore, from that something, I shall make many — with magic!"

Fabrizio watched intently. The old man rolled back the sleeves of his robe. Nothing hidden. He showed the backs of his hands. Nothing there, either. He extended his right hand toward his audience. Empty. His bare left hand gestured as if sculpting air. Suddenly, he was holding a large tarot card that bore the image of a crowned head!

"The king!" exclaimed Mangus, holding the card aloft. "Our beloved Claudio the Thirteenth!"

Fabrizio was astonished.

The crowd — and Fabrizio — applauded wildly.

Mangus offered a courtly bow. "And now," he said, waving his right hand around, "may the king's power — *increase*!"

In an instant *two* tarot cards were in his hand.

Fabrizio laughed. *What wonderful magic!*

Mangus made yet another hand flourish.

*Three* cards were in his hand!

*Four!*

*Five!*

Fabrizio was bedazzled.

"From nothing," proclaimed Mangus, "comes something. From something, many!" With eyes full of merriment, he held up the five tarot cards.

"Bravo!" shouted an excited Fabrizio from the back of the room. "Bravo!"

The crowd joined in.

With another wave of his hands, Mangus made a quick pass. The cards *vanished*!

"Fantastic!" came loud cries from the audience. "Mangus the Magnificent!"

"Oh, I do love magic," whispered Fabrizio, applauding so hard his hands hurt. "My master is truly amazing!"

The old man held up a hand. The crowd hushed.

"Dear friends, thank you kindly. Since magic makes a magician weary, that's all I can do for you tonight. Be assured I shall recover soon enough to perform again — right here — in the near future.

"But now the king's curfew is almost upon us. The king loves us and wishes to keep us safe from devils. Besides, I don't want any of you to sit in one of Count Scarazoni's jail cells."

Somebody hissed.

"I beg you, return to the safety of your homes. But if — *if* — you have found some mystery, some amusement in what I've done, be so kind as to drop a coin or two — a single *pezolla* will be fine — into my servant's cap. No coin is too small! The boy — his name is Fabrizio — stands by the door, cap in hand."

15

Fabrizio grinned with delight.

"Thank you, dear friends," Mangus concluded. "Remember, even a magician must eat!" With a final bow, he stepped behind the backdrop.

That was Fabrizio's cue! He leaped off the basket, scurried to the room's doorway, whipped off his wool cap, and held it before him. The crowd, babbling with pleasure, shuffled toward the exit where he stood.

"Thank you, Signore," Fabrizio said as coins clinked into his cap, one after another. "Thank you, Signora."

Intent on making sure no one took any money out of the cap, Fabrizio paid little attention to those who passed. Only when he decided that the last of the audience had gone did he look up.

He gasped. A large man wrapped in a black robe with the hood hiding most of his face loomed over him. Even as Fabrizio started back, the person grasped him firmly by a shoulder and drew him close.

"Boy!" he whispered harshly. "Tell your master he's in grave danger."

Before Fabrizio could collect his wits, the black robe fled into the night.

Fabrizio gazed at the doorway through which the black robe had fled. *Is that the same man who stood outside our house this morning? What is he warning Master about?*

He was still staring when he heard, "Hey! You! Boy!"

Fabrizio spun around.

Giuseppe, the older of Mangus's two manservants, had stuck his head through a slit in the yellow backdrop. He was about the same size and build as Mangus but bore a head of curly hair and a thick black beard. "Is the audience gone?"

"Yes, Signore," Fabrizio replied. "Everybody."

"Good." Giuseppe pulled aside the backdrop. Mangus, his hat set aside, sat slumped in a chair. Benito, Mangus's other manservant, was already packing up the large props. Benito was quite tall, and liked to show off his strength.

"Fabrizio," Mangus called across the room. "Did we collect much money?"

"Forgive me, Master. You know I can't do sums."

"Alas, I do know."

"But listen!" Fabrizio held up his cap and shook it. He grinned as the coins rattled.

Mangus turned to his other servants. "They say the sound of money is the devil's own laughter. But while there may be too much devil's laughter in the world, there never seems to be enough money."

Benito and Giuseppe looked at each other and laughed loudly.

"Two hungry young men for servants," Mangus continued. "A hungry wife. And I suppose, even a magician must eat."

Fabrizio — aware that he had not been included in the list — approached the magician with cap in hand. "Master, I once heard a priest proclaim that those who can't speak for themselves have the greatest hunger of all."

Benito put the backdrop curtain into a wooden chest and looked around. "Boy! Don't contradict Master!"

Fearful he had been too familiar, Fabrizio held still. "Forgive me, Master," he whispered. "I meant no offense. But, Master, just now, at the door, a man —"

"The money, Fabrizio," interrupted Mangus, his voice heavy with fatigue. "The money."

Fabrizio, deciding it best not to speak just now about the threat, knelt and offered up his cap. Mangus spread his legs so his robe made a bowl into which he dumped the coins. As the magician counted them, Fabrizio eased off the old man's Turkish slippers and began to rub his feet.

"Benito! Giuseppe!" exclaimed Mangus. "I believe we've collected decent earnings for our night's work. But, as your master, it's my duty to inform you: An artist's life is not always successful."

Fabrizio looked up. "Surely, Master, you're not just an artist but a great magician."

Benito, squaring off the tarot cards, snorted with disdain. "There you are, Master: A whole month with us and the ragpicker still believes your magic is real."

"Is that true, Fabrizio?" said a frowning Mangus. He dropped the coins into the leather purse attached to his belt. "Do you really think what I do is true sorcery?"

"No doubt, Master."

Giuseppe snorted. "You see what a fool he is, Master!"

"Fabrizio," said Mangus, "your faith in me is based on ignorance."

Fabrizio, his cheeks burning, handed the old man's slippers to Giuseppe. In return he received a pair of soft boots, which he slipped onto his master's feet. After a moment he looked up. "With permission, Master," he whispered, "I should like to be a magician, too."

"Now that," said Mangus, "would take real magic."

Fabrizio hung his head to hide his stinging tears.

Mangus pulled his feet from the boy's grasp. "Time for home. The king's curfew applies to us, too. I doubt the night watch will look kindly on an elderly charlatan and his cheap tricks."

He started to rise, faltered, and settled back. Fabrizio, still on his knees, shuffled closer to allow the old man to put a hand on his shoulder as an aid to standing.

Giuseppe scowled at him, and then took up the chest at one end. Benito lifted the other. The two servants left the room.

Mangus and Fabrizio followed.

In the tavern's main room, Signor Galda, the pole-thin and balding owner of the tavern, met them. He held out

Mangus's thick wool cloak and affectionately draped it over the old man's shoulders.

"Was it a good performance, Signore?"

"Excellent," said Mangus, patting his purse. "And as always, gracious thanks for letting me use your room."

"Ah, Signore," returned the tavern owner, "it's my pleasure. A goodly number of those who come to see you also eat and drink, so please, continue to perform here. Just send a servant on ahead to give me warning. This is your new boy, I presume."

Fabrizio beamed.

"To be sure," said Mangus. "I'll send someone."

*Someone?* Fabrizio winced. *Oh, please, Mistress,* he thought, *come back before Master discharges me.*

Mangus and Signor Galda exchanged a warm embrace, after which the old man and Fabrizio stepped onto the dark, blustery street. Benito and Giuseppe, twenty steps ahead with the chest, held up a fluttering torch to illuminate the narrow, stone-paved way.

"With permission, Master," said Fabrizio as he reached

up and adjusted the cloak around his master's neck. "You need to keep warm."

Mangus frowned and set off at a slow pace.

Fabrizio stayed close. "Forgive me, Master. Mistress Sophia said I should look after you."

"I can take care of myself," muttered Mangus.

They walked on a few paces until Fabrizio, trying to coax Mangus into talking, said, "Master, your magic tonight was truly wonderful. That last piece — making something from nothing, and then many things — was fantastic. The whole town will be talking."

"Let's hope not," said Mangus. "Not only is the king deeply superstitious, he has outlawed magic. If his authorities learn what I do, they might, like you, believe I make real magic. I could find myself in trouble."

"Master, I know that not all you perform is real magic. But much is."

"There's no such thing as magic," insisted Mangus. "My skill is the ability to fool people into believing what I do is true. I do *imitation* magic — *illusions.* Like my costume, it's just visual nonsense. Performing tricks is the way I put food on my table."

"But, Master, if you had lived on the streets as I did, you'd know that if you didn't read the magic of the clouds, you couldn't forecast the weather. And if you didn't understand the magic of the sea, you couldn't catch fish. And the stars, Master, if you don't know how they move through the heavens, or . . . or how to read tarot cards, you couldn't predict the future."

"Fabrizio, do you really believe such superstitions?"

"Of course, Master, surely."

"Then what is your future?"

"I pray it's with you, Master," whispered Fabrizio.

"Fabrizio," said an exasperated Mangus, "if you wish to remain in my household, know that my real love is philosophy, which is to say, reason and logic, *not* magic! Remember that."

Fabrizio was quiet for a few moments. "Master," he suddenly said. "I just remembered something! When I was collecting coins at the door, someone whispered something strange into my ear."

"Which was?"

"He said, 'Tell your master he's in grave danger.'"

Mangus halted. "What! Who was this person?"

"Forgive me, Master, I have no idea."

"You should have told me sooner. Describe him."

"Master," said Fabrizio. "I was so surprised by his words, and his hasty departure, I can't say what he looked like."

"Was he short?" demanded Mangus. "Tall?"

"Much taller than me. Wrapped in a black robe with his face hidden in his hood."

"Fabrizio, Pergamontio is full of black robes: priests, monks, nuns."

"I just remembered something else: There was another black robe at our door this morning."

"This *morning*?"

"I told him about your performance."

"Why?"

"I was excited about going."

"As far as I recall, there was only one black robe in the audience," said Mangus. "Did you see more?"

"I don't think so."

"Well, then, was the person at our door the same one who gave you the warning?"

"I don't know," said Fabrizio, wishing Mangus's angry eyes did not remind him so much of the skull's eyes.

"Fabrizio, pay attention to what's visible and you can discover what's hidden. The one who spoke to you at the performance: Was his robe *all* you noticed?"

Fabrizio was afraid to look up. "Forgive me. I was surprised by what he said. I suppose to be surprised is to lose one's wits."

"The great blessing, Fabrizio, of having wits," chided Mangus, "is *not* to be surprised. *Omne ignotum pro magnifico!*"

"Is that a magic spell, Master?"

"It's a Latin expression that means 'Everything surprises if we lack knowledge of it.'"

"I always thought that being surprised is the most unsurprising fate of man."

Mangus looked around at the boy. "Who told you that?"

"It's only what I've heard and seen. When you are a homeless orphan — as I was — the teachers God provides are one's own eyes and ears."

"True enough," murmured Mangus.

After they had walked awhile, Fabrizio said, "Master, are you in danger?"

"As I told you, King Claudio is terribly superstitious. He believes in magic and devils. His son, Prince Cosimo, holds to the same nonsense. Be advised: Fear most those who are fearful.

"But, while the heir to the throne is Cosimo, the real power in the kingdom belongs to Count Scarazoni. It's said he's not superstitious. But the gossip is that the prince and the count are rivals."

"During your performance you spoke kindly of the king."

"Fabrizio," Mangus cautioned, "a prudent man speaks differently inside and outside."

"Master, why don't you use your magic to make the unpleasant people . . . vanish?"

Mangus halted. "Fabrizio, once and for all, put magic

out of your head! It's not just folly, it's dangerous! And if you paid attention to the real world, you would have noticed that we've arrived home."

"Forgive me, Master," said Fabrizio, rushing forward to open the door of the old, two-story, timbered house.

As soon as Mangus was inside, Fabrizio bolted the door behind them.

An hour later, Fabrizio lay on his straw pallet in his small loft space thinking about his master's performance. How thrilling it had been! How he wished he could do such magic! He recalled Mistress Sophia's words: "Make Master Mangus love you as much as I do."

*But what can I do when Master doesn't even like me?*

Then Fabrizio thought about the warning that had come from the black robe. If Master was in danger, perhaps he could protect him. Surely Master would love him then. He almost hoped that danger would come.

# CHAPTER 5

$T$WO DAYS LATER, THE MORNING PROVED COLD. FABRIZIO, eager to be at his reading lesson before Mangus reached the study, raced through the household tasks. He warmed his master's room, brought in wood, lit the fire, swept the hall steps and street, emptied the slop bucket, dumped the refuse, brought in water from the street fountain, and sprinkled new rushes on the floors. Then he dashed around the corner to Signor Loti's store to purchase olive oil, which he placed in the back kitchen. Finally, he burst into Mangus's study.

"You're late," said Mangus without lifting his eyes from his reading.

The old man, seated at his table, wore a multilayered woolen robe and old slippers. Half gloves left his fingers unencumbered, the better to turn the pages of his book. A cap covered his head.

"Forgive me, Master," said Fabrizio, standing by the doorway, breath misting in the chilly air. "Since Mistress is gone I've taken on a few of her tasks."

Mangus nodded but said nothing.

Frustrated, Fabrizio went to the lectern and stared at his reading task for the week: a page from the poet Dante. During the past two days he had managed to read only six lines.

Fabrizio blew on his fingertips to warm them. As far as he was concerned, the letters on the page — each one written by hand — were as heavy as stones. He would have to lift them one by one.

He gazed at the first word of the seventh line. His heart sank. It was not a word he knew. He rubbed his eyes, twisted his fingers, and shifted his feet. Wishing help, he stole a glance at Mangus. His master was absorbed in his book. The skull lamp beside him seemed to glare at Fabrizio.

Fabrizio turned back to the page and made himself sound out each letter over and over again — "De . . . De . . . ath. Death!" When he finally grasped the word's meaning, he was exhausted.

He looked about. There had to be more words in that room than in the rest of the world combined. It was as if he were at the bottom of a well of words. Glancing at his master, he wished for the millionth time he would teach him not reading but magic.

Shifting so his back was to Mangus, Fabrizio took a few small *pezollas* from his pocket. He passed them back and forth under the lectern, practicing making them vanish from view.

"Fabrizio!" called Mangus. "Attend to your reading!"

Hastily putting away the coins, Fabrizio whispered, "With permission, Master, may I speak?"

"If a fool speaks," the magician growled while continuing to read from his book, "fools will be found who listen."

Fabrizio tried to think of something that might engage Mangus. "Master, I've heard it said that reading deadens the soul."

"Nonsense," snapped Mangus. "If you are not well read, you might as well *be* dead."

"But, Master, some suggest that too much reading causes blindness."

Mangus looked up. "The wise person knows that reading books is the best way to see the world."

"I give thanks, then," said Fabrizio, "that you have all

the books in the world. As soon as I get through yours, I'll never have to read another."

"There can never be enough books," said Mangus. "The pity is it takes years to create each one."

"Is that true?" said the surprised boy.

"Fabrizio, a book must first be written. To do so, the writer exchanges days for words, months for paragraphs, and years for chapters — time turned into books. There's your magic.

"Then," Mangus continued, "that book must be copied with a fair hand. The result? No two are ever alike. That's why books are full of mistakes. Visit a scriptorium. You'll see how many men and months it takes to copy one volume.

"Even so, the book, once copied, must be illustrated. And bound. In short, it takes vast work and time to make a single tome. Indeed, a book can take as long to be copied as to be written. Wherefore so few volumes. If you are ever fortunate enough to go to school, you'll have to copy your own texts."

In his head Fabrizio vowed never to go to such a ghastly place. But all he said was, "No wonder reading is so hard."

"In your case it's merely your hard head that makes reading difficult."

"Then why insist I learn, Master?"

"Would you like the world to be one color?"

"I suppose not. Everything would be like mud."

"The same for thought and speech," said Mangus. "Reading provides you with words — like the colors of God's rainbow — to paint your ideas, to give beauty and variety to thought. Be advised," the old man said sternly, "I'll keep no ignorant servants in my house."

"Master," Fabrizio whispered. "I'd rather learn magic."

"Your learning to read will be magic enough."

"I'm trying to learn one trick," offered Fabrizio. "How to make coins vanish."

"Every boy who eats knows that trick." Mangus touched the books around him with affection. "Here is Plato. Aristotle. Petrarch. Boccaccio. The sublime Dante sits before you. Fabrizio, these are the world's true magicians. Learn to read them and all mysteries shall be revealed." Curbing his enthusiasm, the magician said, "Enough! Attend to your reading."

Fabrizio sighed. "Perhaps Signori Benito and Giuseppe need me."

"They went off to the market. Now, in the name of heaven, Fabrizio, let me read! And you —"

Thudding erupted on the front door.

"Shall I see who's there, Master?" Fabrizio had already sprung away from the lectern and was heading for the door.

"Stop! I don't wish to see anyone. Send whoever it is away."

"Yes, Master."

Fabrizio ran down the hallway and unbolted the door. Before him stood a very stout man. His face was round, with moist, cowlike eyes, a bulbous nose with hairy nostrils, soft, puffy cheeks, and a grizzled chin. He was wheezing, and the stench of garlic spewed from his loose, thick-lipped mouth. But his bright blue robe — trimmed with white rabbit fur — proclaimed him as a lofty member of the legal profession. Moreover, behind him stood a blue-coated law-court soldier with a sharp pike in hand.

Fabrizio made a bow. "May I be of service, Signore?"

"I," the man bellowed while waving his hands around

like an excited windmill, "am Signor Brutus Lucian DeLaBina, Primo Magistrato of Pergamontio! In charge of all law in our glorious kingdom. I'm here to speak to Mangus the Magician. Take me to him." His strenuous gestures were such that he pulled out a large green handkerchief to mop sweat from his face.

"Signore," said Fabrizio, "with permission, he's reading a book and can't be bothered."

"I assure you," proclaimed the magistrato, shaping his words with his hands, "I am more important than any book! Tell your master if he wishes to remain alive, he will see me — now!"

Startled, Fabrizio said, "Of course, Signore! Let me announce you." He raced back down the hallway and stuck his head into Mangus's study.

"Master," he whispered, "a large, loud, and pompous signore in a blue robe demands to see you."

Mangus kept reading. "The last person I want to see is a lawyer."

"Yes, Master. But . . . this man said you will see him if you wish to remain alive."

Mangus looked up. "Who is this absurd person?"

"Primo Magistrato Brutus Lucian DeLaBina."

"DeLaBina?" Mangus cried, his face turning gray. "Here?" He covered the book he was reading with a sheet of parchment.

"Master, is he trouble?"

"He's Pergamontio's chief prosecutor," said Mangus in an agitated voice, "in charge of all laws and licenses. He presides over the Hall of Justice like a hunting dog, sniffing out whatever *he* deems evil and chewing it up without mercy."

"Master, is this what you were warned about two nights ago?"

"Let's hope not!"

"Shall I send him away?"

"Fabrizio! If the primo magistrato comes to my door, I've no choice but to see him. Lead him in. Quickly! The greater the pomposity, the less the patience."

"Yes, Master," said an alarmed Fabrizio, tearing back to the front door.

# CHAPTER 4

With Fabrizio right behind him, a wheezing DeLaBina stomped loudly into the magician's room. The moment he appeared, Mangus, cap in hand, stood up and bowed.

"Signor Magistrato, you honor me greatly."

"Silence!" proclaimed DeLaBina. He held up a fat hand as if testing the wind.

Fabrizio, surprised to see his master so deferential, edged around the table to be near. Simultaneously, he kept his eyes on DeLaBina, who was looking about the room as if in search of something.

"Signor Magician, you keep a disorderly place."

"It will do for the likes of me, Signor Magistrato."

"It will do for *hiding* things," DeLaBina sneered. "Are all these papers and books about black magic?"

"Signore," said Mangus, "you will search in vain for even one book of black magic. My books were written by great philosophers. To be sure, you will find a few books that teach magic *tricks*, the illusions I perform as a way of earning bread for my household. Children's entertainment, you might say. For the ignorant."

Fabrizio, sensing his master's increasing distress, was becoming upset.

"So you claim," said DeLaBina, waving away such notions with a sweep of his hand. "But the world knows magic as the work of the devil. Indeed, Mangus" — he wagged a finger — "I have heard rumors that you are engaged in *that* kind of magic. Be aware! King Claudio insists that all magic be suppressed. The penalty for practicing it is death."

A trembling Mangus bowed. "Signore, I can assure you, my sole interests are truth and logic, which is to say, reason."

"Just know," retorted DeLaBina, "I have *reasons* to keep my eyes on you, because . . ."

Fabrizio waited for DeLaBina to conclude the sentence. But it was Mangus who said, "Signore, I beg you, be kind enough to tell me why you've graced me with a visit."

"Be seated," commanded DeLaBina.

"Fabrizio!" called Mangus. "A chair!"

Fabrizio darted forward to bring the chair. The magistrato all but fell into it, drew up his bulk to Mangus's table, and then leaned over it as if to take possession. Noticing the lit skull, he backed away.

Fabrizio hurriedly returned to his master's side.

DeLaBina reached into his blue robe and slowly drew out a sheet of paper. Fabrizio could see it had bold writing on it.

"Be so good as to examine this," said the magistrato. As he offered the paper to Mangus, DeLaBina fixed his eyes on the old man's face, as if reading it.

Mangus took the paper into his hands. "It's in Italian, not Latin."

"Vulgar tongue, Italian," scoffed DeLaBina. "Go on, read it out loud."

Mangus did so:

Citizens!

Pergamontio is ruled by weakness!

The kingdom needs a strong ruler!

Establish true authority!

Do not fear a change!

"God protect us!" cried Mangus. He dropped the paper as if it were on fire. "Treason!"

"All change is treason," proclaimed DeLaBina, slapping the table to make his point. "Indeed, whispers of wicked plots to overthrow the king fly about the city like a confetti storm."

"Are they true?" said Mangus.

The magistrato puffed a blast of garlic breath. "That you, Signor Mangus, who consider yourself a man of knowledge, should be deaf to these rumors — which everyone else has heard — says much about the value of your so-called reasoning." He leaned forward. "May I suggest that to always have your nose in a book is no different from having your foot in the grave." He poked a fat finger onto the paper. "Note the last phrase, 'Do not fear a change!' means someone wishes to depose King Claudio and take the crown!"

Fabrizio's eyes grew wide.

"Great heaven!" cried Mangus. "When did this paper appear?"

"Yesterday," said DeLaBina.

"Dreadful," muttered Mangus.

"Indeed," said DeLaBina. "The words inscribed on that paper *are* vile. But, much more important" — the magistrato spoke as if to divulge a secret — "please tell me, Signor Mangus, what do you make of the *hand* that wrote those words?" Looking smug, the magistrato sat back in his chair and swabbed his spittled chin with his handkerchief.

"The *hand*?" said Mangus.

"The *way* it was written!" roared DeLaBina.

Wincing, Mangus darted a baffled look at the man, but drew the skull lantern closer to examine the paper under better light.

Fabrizio edged closer, too.

"It's the work of an inept scribe," Mangus began momentarily. "The hook on the *e* here — and here — is smudged. The descender on the letter *p* has a weak serif. As for the ball on the letter *y*, it's anything but round."

"Which is to say," said DeLaBina, his voice as careful as a hunter setting a trap, "the writing has, shall we agree, a *distinctive* hand?"

"Distinctive of a kind," agreed Mangus, still gazing at the paper. "Rather rough. Not artistic. Indeed, inept. A hand that wrote in haste, perhaps." He looked up. "Happily, not an inscription likely to be repeated."

"Then what," pounced DeLaBina, "do you make of *this*?" He drew out another sheet of paper and flung it at the magician.

Mangus studied the new paper while Fabrizio leaned over to see, too. To his eyes the second paper seemed much like the first.

"Magistrato," said Mangus, "unless my eyes have grown weak, this second sheet appears to contain the same errors of penmanship as the first."

"Indeed. Now consider *these*!" DeLaBina tossed a whole sheaf of papers onto the table.

A startled Mangus spread out the papers and examined them in silence. So did Fabrizio. The sole sound in the room was DeLaBina's spittled and labored breathing.

The magician looked up. "Signore, they are *remarkably* the same. In fact, I should say they are *precisely* the same."

DeLaBina nodded smugly. "Therefore, my question to

you must be, how can such handwriting — on so *many different* sheets of paper — all be *precisely* the same?"

Fabrizio looked to Mangus for his answer.

The old man scratched his beard and pulled his right ear. "I confess I've no idea. Every scribe has his own personality. His quirks. But for so many hands to make the same exact mistakes is . . . uncanny. I can't make sense of it."

"Signor Mangus," cried DeLaBina, pumping the air with a fist, "Pergamontio has been flooded with these treasonous sheets!"

*"Flooded?"*

"Hundreds! Bad enough that they exist. Dreadful for what they say. Far, far worse is the fact that they are all *precisely the same*!"

"It is astonishing," murmured Mangus.

"More than astonishing!" shouted DeLaBina, banging his fist on the table so that the skull — and Fabrizio — jumped. "Such identical replication is impossible for human hands! Not even God — in all his greatness — makes two things alike."

Mangus sat back and shook his head. "Signore, how can it be explained?"

"*I* can explain it!" shouted DeLaBina.

"Then, Magistrato," said an increasingly tense Mangus, "enlighten my ignorance by telling me how such can be."

DeLaBina took a deep breath, rather like — Fabrizio thought — a frog about to jump. "Consider that the king, with my unceasing help, has been successful in keeping Pergamontio free of all modern ideas, technologies, and heresies. Consider what is said on these papers — treason! Consider that these papers speak against His Majesty who is king of Pergamontio by nothing less than the choice of God. Consider that these papers exist in extraordinary numbers throughout the city. *Finally*, consider that such inept work repeats itself with magical exactitude. *Diabolical* exactitude! In short, these vile sheets were made . . . magically. And they were done at the behest of none other than — the devil!"

"The devil?" cried Mangus with astonishment.

"The devil?" echoed Fabrizio.

"Or at the least," said DeLaBina slyly, "some . . . devil-ish person."

"But —"

"Mangus," cried the magistrato, "did you not make magic the other evening at the Sign of the Crown? Did you not inform the crowd that you could, I quote, 'create something from nothing'? And, 'from that something, make many'? And did you not *do* all that — *magically*?"

Fabrizio was amazed the magistrato knew what had occurred.

"How many faces of our king did you make appear — *magically* — in your empty hand? *Five!*" DeLaBina bellowed, answering his own question. "Then, what did you do with our beloved king? You had the intent — one might even say the *treasonous* design — of making him . . . magically . . . *vanish*! As if . . . as if he were — overthrown!"

Mangus opened his mouth. No sound came out.

"Magician," shouted DeLaBina, "admit it! You made multiple copies from nothing — *magically*! And *these* papers appeared *magically* throughout the city the very next day *after* your performance in *precisely* the same fashion! *Magically!*"

"But . . ." said a bewildered Mangus.

Abruptly, DeLaBina pointed at Fabrizio. "You, boy! Were you with your master that night?"

Taken aback to be addressed, Fabrizio said, "Y . . . yes, Signore, I was."

"Did or did not Mangus *make* magic?"

Fabrizio looked to his master.

"Speak the truth, Fabrizio!"

Fabrizio turned back to DeLaBina and stammered, "Y . . . yes, Signore. My master . . . made magic."

"And," prompted DeLaBina, "did he not create *many* images of our king? Something . . . from nothing?"

Fabrizio swallowed twice and whispered, "Yes, Signore, but —"

"Yes!" cried DeLaBina with triumph, thrusting a fat finger toward Mangus as if to pierce him with a sword. "Signor Magician, I have *compelled* your servant to confess the truth. Which is to say that you, Signor Magician, made many exact copies from nothing — *magically!*"

"Signore —"

"I sum up: Nobody else in Pergamontio can make magic but you. These papers were made magically. *Ergo*, no one else but you could have made these papers."

"But it's not true," protested Mangus.

"It *is* true," declared DeLaBina. "But," his voice softened, "I can see no reason why such a lowly person — such as you — would want to depose King Claudio. It has to be that you made these papers, foolishly, at the request of some devilish . . . person.

"As punishment for such an act," DeLaBina roared on, "I, the primary law officer of this glorious kingdom, have decreed that *you* shall reveal the malefactor behind this vile conspiracy to depose the king. In short, *you*, Master Magician, shall have the honor of saving . . . the king!"

"But, Magistrato, the notion that I could —"

"Master Mangus," said DeLaBina, heaving himself to his feet so that to Fabrizio's eyes he seemed to fill the room, "I suppose even *you* can see the logic and reason of my words."

Fabrizio watched with dismay as Mangus slumped down, defeated.

DeLaBina gathered his robe around him with a showy swirl. Then he held up his hand and counted upon his fat fingers. "Signor Mangus, you are hereby commanded to do three things.

"One: Rid the city of these treasonous papers.

"Two: Reveal the devilish person who asked you to make these papers magically in order to depose King Claudio.

"Three: Inform me who that person is, so I may inform the king, who will, no doubt, burn this person at the stake."

"Me?" stammered Mangus. "Do . . . all . . . that?"

"Do those three things and you will preserve your life. *Fail* to do them and I, Signor Brutus Lucian DeLaBina, Primo Magistrato of Pergamontio, will be forced to conclude that *you*, Master Mangus, *are the sole traitor*!"

"But, Magistrato," said Mangus, struggling to his feet, "my performance consisted of . . . of illusions. Nothing at all to do with these papers."

"Signore," pleaded Fabrizio, "my master is innocent."

"Innocent?" roared DeLaBina. "You already confessed he made magic!"

Fabrizio was horrified.

"Master Magician," said DeLaBina, "I repeat, if you do *not* reveal the traitor behind this wicked plot, the kingdom of Pergamontio shall require the *illusion* of justice. In other words, I shall find *someone* to burn for this treason! And that person shall be you. Do I make myself perfectly clear?"

"Signore," whispered Mangus as he slumped back into his chair, "I fear you have."

After seeing DeLaBina out, Fabrizio raced back to his master's study and flung himself onto his knees. "Master, forgive me!"

Mangus, who had spread the treasonous papers out before him, looked down at the boy. "Forgive you? For what?"

"I told that man the truth about your magic."

"What you did," said an angry Mangus, "was to confuse what you *think* is true with what *is* true."

Fabrizio put a hand to his heart. "Thank you for correcting me, Master. From now on I shall only think untrue things."

"No! Always speak the truth."

"Even if it harms you?"

"Fabrizio, philosophy teaches that truth neither helps nor hinders. What matters is the way you deal with it."

"Yes, Master. From now on I'll only tell the truth when it helps you."

"Fabrizio," cried an exasperated Mangus, "only fools think themselves wise! A wise man knows his ignorance."

"Then I must be the smartest person in the whole world because I'm the stupidest!"

"Fabrizio, get off your knees and stop your nonsense! This business" — Mangus waved his hand over the papers — "is deadly serious."

Fabrizio stood. "Master, I beg you, don't do what that man asked. You know what people say: Seek the devil and he'll find you first."

"I've no intention of seeking the devil."

"But the magistrato said these papers were the devil's work."

"You may be sure the devil is not interested in such a wretched place as Pergamontio. No, these papers are the work of some human who wishes to depose the king. I assure you, there is no devil involved."

"Master, everybody knows there are devils everywhere who —"

"Stop! If you had listened carefully, you would have

understood. DeLaBina claimed I made the papers *magically*. Yes. But he went on to say that some *devilish* person — not the devil — *requested* them. That person is the one DeLaBina is after.

"But," said Mangus, gazing at the papers, "I have no choice. It's I who must find the one who made them. A command from the primo magistrato is a command from the king. Or worse, Count Scarazoni. If I can't find the one who made these ghastly papers, the magistrato will blame me."

"But why?"

"Because — and heed me well, Fabrizio — though truth is reason, the truth is rarely seen as reasonable." Mangus pressed his hands against his temples.

Fabrizio watched him for a moment. "Master, why don't you use your magic to solve the problem?"

"Fabrizio," yelled Mangus, "once and for all, I have no magic!"

"Yes, Master," said Fabrizio, backing away and bobbing a bow three times. "Of course, Master. Whatever you say, Master."

Mangus closed his eyes. "Still, that such a hand —
even a poor hand — can replicate itself with extreme
exactitude, that, truly, is a . . . mystery."

Fabrizio waited a few moments before asking, "What
can you do, Master?"

Mangus glared at the boy. "God gave us the gift of reason. To use it, Fabrizio, is our gift to him. Unfortunately,
the enemy of reason is exhaustion, and though it's still early
in the day, I'm already weary." He closed his eyes.

"Master," whispered Fabrizio, "if you can't find the . . .
traitor, will they really . . . burn you?"

"That's what he threatened."

Fabrizio stared at his master. The thought of him suf-
fering such a fate made him sick. He fetched and draped a
shawl over the old man's shoulders.

"Master, I know you think me a fool and wish I'd
never come into your home. But please, I beg you, let
me help."

"You're nothing but an ignorant street beggar."

Fabrizio hung his head.

Mangus glanced up at the boy, shifted uncomfortably in his chair, and said, "Well . . . tell me, then. What would you do?"

Fabrizio thought desperately. "I could . . . I could go about the city and gather up the papers until there are no more. Wasn't that the first thing that DeLaBina asked of you?"

"I suppose such an effort would at least keep you from jabbering into my ear. Fine. Go and try to collect the papers."

"Yes, Master, and . . . and should I ask people where they came from? Who they thought made them?"

"Any clue will help," conceded Mangus.

"I'll pray I find one," said Fabrizio. He started for the door.

"Fabrizio!" called Mangus. "Do not forget: DeLaBina's spies and informers are everywhere. Do nothing to bring suspicion on me. Speak to no one about the accusations. Do you hear me? *No one!*"

Fabrizio ran back, snatched up Mangus's hand, and

kissed it. "Master, as I am loving to you and your name, I'll do just what you ask."

Mangus sighed. "I'll take comfort in the thought that all beginnings are fueled by hope."

"Master, on the street people say, 'Though hope is bright as fire, it can't boil water.'"

"For God's sake, Fabrizio!" cried Mangus. "Leave me!"

"Yes, Master," said Fabrizio. "Just know that I'm trying to help you." He bowed five times and then ran out of the room.

# CHAPTER 6

As Fabrizio rushed down the hallway, he crashed into Benito and Giuseppe. The two servants were just entering the house.

"Stupid boy!" shouted Giuseppe. "Look where you're going!"

"Signori," said Fabrizio, noting their empty hands. "I thought you were at market and —"

"It's none of your business where we were," said Giuseppe, leaning over the boy. "Where are you going?"

"It's Master, he —" Suddenly remembering that Mangus had told him not to speak to anyone about the matter, Fabrizio slapped a hand over his mouth.

Benito pulled it away. "Has something happened?"

"Well, yes, or rather, no. Maybe. With permission, I hope not."

"What is it?" demanded Giuseppe.

Fabrizio darted a nervous glance back toward Mangus's study. "Forgive me, Signori," he whispered. "Master told me not to tell anyone."

"We are not anyone," said Benito, slapping Fabrizio's ear from behind. "We're your betters."

The boy bowed his head and murmured, "Yes, Signore, whatever you say."

Giuseppe boxed Fabrizio's other ear. "With Mistress not here to coddle you, you'll do as *we* tell you."

Fabrizio, remembering Mistress Sophia's request that he not quarrel with the servants, pressed back against the wall and averted his eyes. "I'm just trying to help Master."

"You can start by telling us everything about this matter," said Giuseppe. "Now come with us!"

"But, Master told me —"

"Blockhead!" said Benito. "It's not Master or Mistress who manages things here, but us."

Wishing he were twice as big and three times stronger, Fabrizio followed Benito out through the back of the house. They passed through a small courtyard where some of Mangus's larger magic apparatuses were stored: multicolored chests. A huge jar. A large pine coffin with fancy iron handles. Fabrizio knew they were used for appearances and disappearances, none of which Fabrizio had seen his master perform. He paused at the coffin, wishing he could jump inside and hide. Giuseppe pushed him on.

On the far side of the courtyard, next to a door that led out into the back alley, stood a small shed. It contained two rooms: the household kitchen and the place in which Benito and Giuseppe lived.

Once inside, Giuseppe turned to Fabrizio. "All right, what's happened with Master?"

"Signore, it's truly a private matter that —"

Benito shoved Fabrizio hard. "Boy, I've been here for years. Giuseppe the same. You have been here one month. Master thinks you're a fool. We agree. In short, you have no rights!"

"Signori," gasped Fabrizio. "I understand: The ocean may be large, but little fish follow the big fish."

"Perfect," said Giuseppe. "Because big fish *eat* smaller fish."

"So tell us what's happened," said Benito. "We need to know. And be quick about it!"

Fabrizio, feeling he had no choice, related what had passed between Magistrato DeLaBina and Mangus.

As he talked, Giuseppe and Benito kept exchanging looks.

"So you see," Fabrizio concluded, "because the magistrato claims Master made those papers with magic and that someone devilish told him to make them, it's Master's duty to reveal the one who got him to do the deed and committed treason."

"Did you truly tell DeLaBina that Master does *real* magic?" asked Giuseppe.

"Signore, Master said I was always to tell the truth."

"Did it ever occur to you," said Benito, "that telling the truth is bad for *us*?"

"The magistrato only said he might punish Master."

"You don't know how the world works, do you?" said Giuseppe. "When masters are punished once, servants are punished twice."

"What has Mangus decided to do about this matter?" asked Benito.

"He has no choice. He must find the one who is trying to depose the king."

Once again Benito and Giuseppe looked at each other.

"How does he intend to do that?" asked Giuseppe.

"To begin, I was going out to collect all the papers."

"*You?*" said Giuseppe.

"Forgive me, Signori, but Mistress Sophia said I was to take care of Master."

"Did she?" said Benito. "Fine! Do so! As for us, we'll take care of ourselves."

"But," said Giuseppe, shaking a fist in Fabrizio's face, "make sure you keep no secrets from us!"

"Now get out of here," yelled Benito, "and do what you promised Master you'd do."

"Yes, Signori," said Fabrizio. "Of course. Absolutely. Small fish! Big fish! True! Untrue! With permission!" And trying to dodge a flurry of blows, he dashed away.

# CHAPTER 7

Fabrizio burst out of the house and onto the narrow cobblestone Street of the Olive Merchants. Sprinting to the first turning, he halted to rub the bruises he had just received. "Nasty Benito," he muttered. "Ugly Giuseppe."

He started to walk. The morning's air, warmed by a golden sun, was dusty and sweet. The smells of new-pressed olive oil, roasting meat, and baking bread soothed him until he gazed up at the mountain looming over Pergamontio. There, perched on its summit, was the Castello, the great fortification where King Claudio, his family, and court resided. Fabrizio could see armed sentries — more than usual — pacing the crenellated walls. Sparks of sunlight glinted off their polished armor.

Fabrizio was grateful he had never been to the Castello. Too many people had been dragged there, never to be seen again, not so much as a bone.

It was all the doing — people claimed — of Count Scarazoni. Perhaps, thought Fabrizio, Magistrato DeLaBina was there right now conferring with the count about Mangus. It was a frightful thought.

Fabrizio lowered his gaze to the street and watched people pass. It took only moments for him to realize something *was* different. Usually, raucous cries were heard everywhere: "Buy my oil!" "Fine figs!" "Lovely pots to be had!" But this day, though men and women, many laden with baskets and dressed in colorful clothing, filled the street like a carnival parade, people appeared sullen and tense, offering little idle or noisy chatter. Rather, they had gathered in small knots, whispering among themselves while furtively glancing over shoulders to see who might be listening. Even the priests, monks, and nuns in their white-, gray-, and black-hooded robes seemed preoccupied, barely greeting passersby as was their custom. As for the regular swarms of children darting here and there like dashing minnows, they were nowhere to be seen. The loudest street noise was a plodding donkey that brayed.

But the streets were full of Count Scarazoni's green-coated soldiers. Armed with pikes and swords, they dispersed every gathering they came upon.

Fabrizio recalled the words on the treasonous paper:

Citizens!

Pergamontio is ruled by weakness!

The kingdom needs a strong ruler!

Establish true authority!

Do not fear a change!

It all made Fabrizio hungry.

At the nearest stall he ordered a square of flat bread with olive oil, garlic, and mashed basil. After he received his food and paid his coin, he leaned forward. "Signore," he whispered, "have you seen any of those papers calling for . . . for change in Pergamontio?"

The man stared. "Be off with you!"

Fabrizio found a sunny spot by a bubbling fountain, sat down, and chewed his bread. All the while he kept an eye out for the papers. Within five minutes, a baker, dusted with flour from hair to foot, came down the street clutching one.

Gulping down the last of his bread, Fabrizio hastened

to follow. "Excuse me! Pardon me!" When he finally caught up with the man, he grabbed his thick arm.

The baker swung around.

"With permission, Signore!" said Fabrizio. "That paper in your hand — where did you get it?"

The man gawked at Fabrizio, flung the paper away, turned, and lumbered off in haste.

Fabrizio retrieved the paper from the gutter. He could not really read it, but he recognized the words: the same paper DeLaBina had brought to Mangus. To see an exact replica there on the street was uncanny. *It does seem magical.*

A quiver of dread passed through him.

Stuffing the paper into his tunic sleeve, he posted himself in a doorway to watch for more of the papers. Within moments he spotted a strolling carpenter reading one.

Fabrizio leaped before him. "Signore! With perfectly friendly intentions, that paper you are reading —"

The man turned red, tossed the paper into Fabrizio's face, and dashed down an alley without looking back.

Fabrizio looked at it. It, too, was the same.

After slipping this second paper up his sleeve, he walked through the city in search of more. He found them in many hands. Whenever he managed to scrutinize them, they were *exactly* the same. And when he asked people where they got them, they replied,

"On my doorstep."

"Stuck to a wall."

"It just appeared."

"How?" demanded Fabrizio.

No one could explain.

For the rest of the afternoon, Fabrizio went about the city collecting the papers. Why, he wondered anew, could not Mangus admit that it must have taken magic to make so many exactly alike?

When he had gathered all the papers he could, Fabrizio felt very pleased with himself. He could not wait to show Mangus that he had achieved the first of the magistrato's tasks. Surely Master would be pleased with him. And Mistress Sophia would be very proud.

Stuffing the papers into his sleeves, Fabrizio set off through the city, taking a shortcut through an alley. He was halfway through when a law-court soldier — in his blue uniform — appeared and blocked the far end.

Startled, Fabrizio stopped.

"You are under arrest for treason!" announced the soldier.

"God protect me!" Spinning around, Fabrizio ran toward the other end of the street only to be confronted by yet another blue coat. Realizing he was trapped, he reached for the papers to get rid of them. Before he could, the soldiers leaped forward and held him fast.

Fabrizio was forced out to the main street. There, waiting on his horse, was Magistrato DeLaBina. With him was a whole troop of blue coats, all with swords in hand.

As soon as he approached DeLaBina, Fabrizio said, "Signor Magistrato, with permission, I have been trying —"

"Silence!" shouted the magistrato. "I know what you've been doing. Search him."

It took just seconds for the soldiers to find the treasonous papers. They handed them up to DeLaBina, who gave them only a cursory glance.

"Exactly as I thought," DeLaBina exclaimed so all could hear. "Proof that Mangus the Magician is making treasonous papers and, with the help of his servant boy, spreading them about the city. Only one question remains. Who is he acting for?"

"Signore . . ." tried Fabrizio.

"Silence!" said DeLaBina. "Take him to the Hall of Justice!"

A soldier yanked Fabrizio onto the back of his horse. As he did, DeLaBina, with a shout, called up his men. The whole troop galloped into motion.

The horses raced around the corner. That was when Fabrizio saw Giuseppe standing by the side of the street. He was smiling.

# CHAPTER 8

$\mathfrak{D}$ELABINA LED THE WAY, GALLOPING THROUGH THE
city's narrow, winding streets, to the Hall of Justice. The
great stone building with its high tower stood on
Pergamontio's main city square, directly opposite the city
cathedral. Fabrizio had always thought it beautiful. Now
all he could think about was that the building bulged with
courts, lawyers' offices, barracks for the law-court soldiers,
as well as many jail cells, and even an executioner. Milling around the entryway was an army of Scarazoni's
green-coated soldiers — more than Fabrizio had ever seen
there before.

The magistrato barked a sharp command. Fabrizio was
yanked from the horse, then made to march swiftly through
the entrance. Its columns made him think of gigantic teeth
and that he was about to be chewed up and swallowed
alive.

At the end of a hall they approached a closed door
guarded by more green-coated soldiers. DeLaBina halted.

"Signor Magistrato!" a court soldier demanded. "What is the password?"

"The King's Justice," said a voice.

Startled, DeLaBina wheeled around. Fabrizio followed the magistrato's look. "My lord," said the magistrato.

Prince Cosimo — the king's elder son and heir to the throne — stepped forward. He was a tall, lanky fellow in his midtwenties, with a boyish pink-cheeked face, pug nose, and a thin wisp of a blond mustache that made him look very young. His clothing was quite elegant: a bright blue jacket with pearl buttons, a golden cloak draped over one shoulder, a purple velvet cap with a long green feather, yellow leggings, red boots, and white gloves.

Fabrizio looked upon him with relief. Perhaps Cosimo, looking kind in nature, would take pity on him. Immediately, he fastened his hopes on him. But the young man ignored Fabrizio and looked only at DeLaBina, offering a tiny nod of recognition. A flustered DeLaBina bowed and blotted the sweat from his bulging neck with his handkerchief.

The prince led the way into a room that made Fabrizio

gasp. It had a lofty, coffered ceiling of intricate wood carving, a display of rich tapestries, large wall paintings, fine furniture, and a whole array of multicolored flags, bloody swords, dented shields, and torn battle banners. Here was a world of vast wealth and power.

DeLaBina grabbed the frightened Fabrizio by the neck and with a kick forced him forward until he stood before a slightly raised platform at the end of the room. There, seated on a bench covered with golden cloth, sat the king of Pergamontio himself — Claudio the Thirteenth.

The king was a short, wide man of middling years. His skin was coarse, his nose thick, his lips — surrounded by a heavy close-cropped gray beard — were frowning. His hands — barnacled with great glittering rings — were large, broad-fingered, and in constant fidget while moist, edgy eyes kept looking now here, now there, as if on alert for an attack that might come at any moment. Indeed, he kept gripping and releasing the ruby-encrusted dagger that hung from his belt. Fabrizio had no doubt: The dagger, despite its jewels, was not merely ornamental.

As Prince Cosimo joined his father and stood on the king's left, Fabrizio kept trying to catch his eye, but to no effect.

Next to Prince Cosimo stood Prince Lorenzo, the king's second and younger son. Fabrizio saw nothing elegant or powerful about him, nothing to suggest he might help.

And then Fabrizio realized that standing on the king's right was Count Scarazoni. Dressed entirely in black, Count Scarazoni had a thin, pinched face with dark eyebrows that swept over his angry eyes like a bar of iron. His mouth was a grim, bloodless line while a sharp, pointed beard shaped his chin. His hands — encased in tight black leather gloves — were balled into fists. A dagger hung from his belt, too. Fabrizio thought him coiled with fury, ready to strike.

There were, Fabrizio knew, a Queen Jovanna and a Princess Teresina, the king and queen's daughter. Neither was present.

Confronted by such riches and magnificence, and all these powerful people staring at him, Fabrizio felt utterly alone. *Why did I ever offer to collect those papers?* he asked himself.

Then he realized that in the king's hand was one of the treasonous papers.

"My lords," bellowed DeLaBina, "I have requested your presence here so I might speak on dangerous matters of state!" He bowed to the king.

Fabrizio, feeling he must do something, bowed as well.

King Claudio had been whispering to Prince Cosimo, showing him the paper. The prince, with nervous care, took the paper in his hands cautiously. Hearing DeLaBina, he looked up. To Fabrizio's surprise, however, it was the count, his face knotted with rage, who called, "Yes, DeLaBina! Why did you ask us to come down here?"

"Your Majesty, noble princes, great count," replied DeLaBina, "vile writings have been circulating throughout the city."

The king shifted uneasily on his bench. "You mean this attack on me?" He pointed to the paper in the prince's hand.

"The same, my lord."

"Which has appeared in such great numbers?" said the count.

"Yes, my lord."

"And circulated freely throughout the city?" the count added.

"Quite true, my lord," said DeLaBina.

"There are those," cried the count, "who apparently would like to depose the king and end his rightful rule! Let me state here and now, that *all* such conspiracies will be crushed without mercy. I don't care whose evil hand concocted this plot." The count glared at DeLaBina. "Anyone — *anyone* — high or low — who so much as touches our anointed king — shall pay a dreadful penalty!" His hand went to his dagger.

Fabrizio trembled at his rage.

King Claudio, white-faced, retreated into a corner of the bench as if wishing to hide. "That's true enough, Count," he said. "We intend to remain on our rightful throne so long as a loving God gives us strength to breathe." In a feeble display of anger, he pulled out his dagger and rested it on his lap.

"And let the world know," Prince Cosimo added, "that I, too, have the strength and will to protect my father." He put one hand on the king's shoulder as if to reassure him, even as he took away the king's dagger, the way a parent might remove a dangerous toy from a child.

"Quite correct, my lords," said DeLaBina, bowing toward the king with almost every syllable he spoke. "I can assure you that His Majesty's Ministry of Justice and Licenses — which I have the honor to command — is here to expose all traitors!"

"And if you don't, I shall," said the prince, looking over the king's head toward the count while putting his father's dagger in his own belt.

It made Fabrizio recall something Mangus had said, that the count and prince were rivals for the king's attention.

"My lord," said DeLaBina, this time speaking directly to the king. "Fear not. I have made much progress in this matter. I've determined that the identical replications of these papers prove they have come from the most evil of malefactors, the heart of sinfulness."

"Ghosts?" cried the king. "Is that who made the papers? Ghosts can do anything they wish, you know. They go everywhere, too. Did they make the papers?"

"Worse," said DeLaBina.

"Worse?" cried the king. "What . . . what could be worse than ghosts?" He gripped the edge of the bench as if to spring up and run.

"My king," said DeLaBina, "considering your importance in this world, it's no wonder that you have attracted an enemy more fearful than ghosts. It is —" He paused dramatically.

"Who?" the king asked, his voice trembling.

"My lord," said DeLaBina, "I fear it is . . . someone in league with the devil."

"God protect me!" shrieked the king.

"Which is to say," DeLaBina hurried on, "someone ordered these treasonous papers to be made — *magically*."

No sooner did DeLaBina say this than the prince — who had been holding the paper — cried out, "*Magic?* God preserve us!" and flung it away as if it were on fire.

"It's just what I've always feared," cried the king. "Malignant spirits — ghosts — devils — hover about Pergamontio and wish to do us harm!" He looked with dismay first at Prince Cosimo and then at Count Scarazoni. "Count Scarazoni. Why have you done nothing about this?"

The count ignored the question and spoke instead to the magistrato. "Signor DeLaBina, do you truly believe these papers were made *magically*?"

"How else can you explain that so many were made exactly the same? So yes, made magically, but ordered by someone."

"Where is this someone?" demanded Count Scarazoni. "If you can bring him forward, I shall cut out his heart!"

*Oh, my poor master!* thought Fabrizio.

"My lord," said DeLaBina, "I won't *guess* where that particular person might be at this moment. For all I know he could be in this room." He stared at Scarazoni. "At this point I only know the individual who actually made these papers."

"Who . . . who might that be?" stammered the alarmed king.

"My lord, it is" — DeLaBina paused for effect — "it is Mangus the Magician!"

Fabrizio groaned inwardly.

The king looked bewildered. "Who?" he demanded.

"He is speaking," said Count Scarazoni, "of a magician who resides in your city."

"A *magician*?" said the king, staring at the count with horror. "Here? In my Pergamontio?"

"He lives on the Street of the Olive Merchants," said Scarazoni.

*How does he know that?* Fabrizio wondered.

"But . . . but magicians are terribly dangerous," said the king. "If you knew of this magician, Count, why did you not inform me?"

"Yes, Count," said the prince, "you seem to know all about this magician."

"*Do* you know about him?" the king demanded of Scarazoni.

"Let us hear what DeLaBina says first," said the count.

The next moment DeLaBina turned and forced Fabrizio into a kneeling position. "My lords, before you is the wretched servant boy of this Mangus the Magician. He goes by the name of . . ."

Before he completed the sentence, Count Scarazoni said, "Fabrizio."

Once again Fabrizio was startled. How could the count know his name?

DeLaBina, equally surprised, recovered quickly. "Apparently, Count, you have considerable knowledge of this magician. I suppose *you* will not be surprised to know that when *I* apprehended this boy, *I* discovered these on him." The magistrato reached into his blue robe and pulled out the papers Fabrizio had collected.

"Your Majesty," continued DeLaBina, "this boy admitted to me that Mangus was practicing magic. The papers I found on him are the same as you held in your hand. One of my informants told me this boy was distributing the papers throughout the city. I caught him in the act."

"Not true, Your Majesty," Fabrizio whispered.

No one even heard him.

"One can hardly imagine," said DeLaBina, "such a stupid, lowborn fellow doing such a thing if he was not following *somebody's* orders."

"Who told the magician to make the papers?" asked the prince.

"I am afraid," said DeLaBina, looking at the count, "there is as yet an unknown accomplice."

The king sat up. "If this magician is *making* these papers, then surely he can tell us who the traitor is. Arrest him. Force him to reveal who asked him to make the papers." He paused and looked at Fabrizio. "Is this boy a . . . magician, too?"

"Of course not," said Scarazoni.

"Good! Then bring him forward. I'll question him right now."

DeLaBina pushed Fabrizio forward with such force that the boy fell to his knees. When he looked up, the king was staring at him with nervous fascination.

"Boy!" cried the king. "Does your master practice magic?"

"Majesty . . . with permission," Fabrizio stammered, "I

humbly, respectfully, and truthfully beg to inform you that my master had nothing to —"

"Does he commune with ghosts?" demanded the king.

"Is he a sorcerer?" asked Prince Cosimo.

"No . . . please," said Fabrizio. "He . . . had nothing to do with —"

"Then tell me who asked him to make the papers."

"Your Majesty . . ."

"Tell me!" cried the king.

Fabrizio was aware everyone was looking at him. Desperate, he searched for a friendly face. He gazed at Prince Cosimo, pleading silently with imploring eyes for help. "I . . . I . . . believe it is —"

Prince Cosimo turned pale. "Father, don't waste your time with this wretch. Since the magician is guilty, take this worthless servant to the lowest dungeon of the Hall of Justice — to the executioner. Have the boy executed within twenty-four hours as an example to all who would threaten us."

"Yes," cried the king. "Lead him away. DeLaBina! Arrest the magician!"

Before a shocked Fabrizio fully grasped what was happening, he was seized by two soldiers and dragged off.

# CHAPTER 9

Two court soldiers, their smoky torches spattering shadows on the walls, marched Fabrizio down steep stone steps. They went around twisty bends, along clammy, spiderwebbed hallways, through narrow, moss-clotted passageways. Every turn confused him. Every step lower terrified him. As far as Fabrizio could tell, he was being taken to the very bottom of the Hall of Justice.

At last they reached the end of a narrow corridor where a bulky wooden door — strapped and studded with black bolts — blocked the way. One of the soldiers used his sword butt to bang on it.

The door swung open. A huge, filth-slathered, pale-skinned man with knobby legs and long-muscled arms peered out. He wore a stained leather smock that reached scabby knees. His feet were bare, with hammertoes that curled upon themselves like claws. To Fabrizio the man looked like a gigantic maggot.

"There you are, Agrippa," said one of the soldiers. "You do take your time."

"Forgive me," said the executioner in a voice that surprised Fabrizio with its mildness. "I get weary sitting here, waiting. Makes a man slow." He blinked. "Have you brought me business?"

"We have."

"Let's have a look." The executioner reached out a heavy hand and shoved one of the soldiers aside. His gray eyes blinked at Fabrizio. Staring up with revulsion, the boy started back.

"Why, he's just a minnow," said Agrippa.

"What do you care?" said a soldier. "Do what you're told: Execute him."

"Who ordered his death?" asked Agrippa.

"Prince Cosimo."

"That's unusual. Mostly it's Scarazoni who sends folk here. What's this tadpole done?"

"Does it matter?" said one of the soldiers.

The executioner shrugged his great shoulders. "I suppose not. What's his sentence?"

"To be executed at the end of twenty-four hours."

"Twenty-four hours! The usual practice is for prisoners

to suffer a week before they are executed. This one must have done something terrible."

"Why should you care?"

"Fine," said Agrippa. "I can save a *pezolla* by not feeding him. Not that such a minnow would eat much." He reached out, but Fabrizio jerked back, trying to break away from the soldiers. They were too quick, and held him. The executioner grabbed the boy by a shoulder and yanked him forward. Fabrizio stumbled into the cell, all but tripping over a corpse that lay upon the ground.

"And take this one out," said Agrippa, indicating the body.

"Is he dead?" asked a soldier.

"I hope so. I broke his neck three days ago."

Sick to his stomach, Fabrizio pressed himself against the far wall.

The soldiers crowded into the small room, grabbed the dead man's legs, and dragged him out, slamming the door behind them.

Fabrizio looked about. The small space was illuminated by a few glowing coals in a rusty iron bucket. Along with the feeble light, the coals oozed caustic smoke that lay like ribbons in the reeking air. The room's walls, low ceiling, and floor were made of crudely cut stone. Wisps of rotten, clotted hay lay scattered. The only bright thing in the room was a large hourglass hanging motionless from a chain affixed to the ceiling. Its bulky bottom bulb was filled with white sand.

All that Fabrizio could think was that just a short time ago he had been snug and safe in Master's house. Now he was in this bleak and desolate place. And there he would remain for twenty-four hours, after which he would be put to a cruel death for no reason at all.

The executioner sat cross-legged on the floor, blocking the door. Arms folded over his massive chest, he continued to examine Fabrizio with curiosity.

Fabrizio, struggling to breathe, said, "Please, Signore. My name is —" only to have Agrippa press one of his large, filthy hands over his mouth.

"I don't want to know your name," the man announced. "Hard enough to execute someone. Knowing names makes it harder." He removed his hand.

The moment he did, Fabrizio cried, "My name is Fabrizio!"

The executioner sighed. "Gory. That always happens. Soon as I tell people *not* to reveal their names, they do. Executioners have feelings, too, you know. Not that anybody cares about making things more difficult for me."

"For you?" said Fabrizio. "What about me?"

Agrippa shrugged. "Your life will be short. Mine longer. Look at it that way, and you'll see it's more of a problem for me than for you. All the same, I'm pleased to meet you, Signor Fabrizio. I sincerely regret our acquaintance will be brief."

"I confess," said Fabrizio, "I'm not pleased to meet you."

He looked around only to notice, with surprise, that the door behind the executioner had been left ajar. His eyes widened.

"You're an alert one," said Agrippa. "Yes, the door is open. I always keep it that way. Gives my prisoners some hope. Hope, I think, is a good thing."

"Hope is a good way to start your dinner but a bad way to finish it," Fabrizio shot back.

"Ah, a clever lad!" Agrippa's grin revealed stumps of yellowing teeth. "But I'm strong. So you won't escape. I mean, you don't want to spend the rest of your life — short though it may be — in pain, do you?"

Fabrizio leaned back against the wall, shut his eyes, and took a deep breath. "An old man once told me that when there's nowhere to go, it's best to stay where you are."

"Don't complain," said Agrippa. "I'll be here much longer than you."

"Don't you like your job?" said Fabrizio.

"When I was your age, I wanted to be a stonemason. Something respectable and everlasting about building homes and walls. Outdoors, too. The good God willed it otherwise, didn't he? Still, I should be grateful for work that keeps me alive."

"Except you stay alive by making others die." Fabrizio pointed to the hourglass. "What's that for?"

"Kind of you to remind me. The sand measures your

remaining time." Agrippa lumbered up and flipped the hourglass over.

"You heard the soldier," he said, resuming his place by the door. "After twenty-four hours you die."

Fabrizio watched the sand trickle down. He turned away.

"Some of my guests," said Agrippa, "want to end things quickly. The guilty ones, mostly. Not the innocent. Odd how optimism and innocence cling together. A depressing connection, if you ask me."

"Do you kill the innocent, too?" asked Fabrizio.

"I'm not a judge, am I?" said Agrippa.

"But if you were, you'd find me innocent. All I wanted to do was help my master. He needs help. If you wished, I'd be happy to beg for mercy."

"Sorry. I'm not a pardoner, either. Just an executioner."

Fabrizio was silent for a while. "How . . . how do you . . . execute people?"

Agrippa held up his large, dirty hands. "I break their necks."

Fabrizio, unable to keep from touching his own neck, watched the thread of sand trickle down. He felt it hard to breathe.

"Unless of course the king decides to send a messenger. A reprieve."

"Does that happen?" asked Fabrizio, eagerly.

"Not once," Agrippa replied. "Still, they say the more a thing hasn't happened, the greater the chances are that it might. But I'll be honest: Your death will more likely take place sooner."

"Sooner!" cried Fabrizio.

"Now that happens a lot. Count Scarazoni gets impatient. But, don't worry. You'll be forewarned. A messenger comes and knocks on this door — loudly. If you hear it — and you're not likely to miss it — pray for your soul. The end is soon."

"Considering what you do, you seem cheerful enough."

"When I first got this job, I said to myself, 'Agrippa, no reason to make things worse for your guests, is there?' A light touch eases the way."

Fabrizio, his teeth chattering, drew up his knees to gather some measure of warmth.

"Look here," said Agrippa, reaching out and rapping Fabrizio on the foot. "I don't have much of a social life. Just when I get to know a fellow, I have to kill him. I'd love a chat. It passes the time. Or would you prefer silence?"

"I'd like the sand to stop."

"No one can stop time. Just tell me, Signor Fabrizio, since I'm your sole remaining friend — what was your crime?"

"*I did nothing!*" Fabrizio shouted.

"No need to yell. I just want you to know I feel it's my obligation to believe anything my guests say. Makes them feel better."

"But I *am* innocent!" Fabrizio covered his face with his hands to keep from seeing the hourglass.

"Then why did Prince Cosimo condemn you to death?"

"I don't know," wailed Fabrizio.

"Maybe he's protecting his father."

89

"I'm protecting my master! But now they're going to arrest him. It's all my fault."

"Now, now, no need for tears," said Agrippa. "Just tell me your story. It usually makes the condemned feel better. I love stories. Never get enough of 'em. Another service I provide. Now go on, let's hear it right from the beginning."

Fabrizio told the details of his life, concluding by saying, "DeLaBina told the king it was my master who made the papers — magically. But I'm beginning to think DeLaBina doesn't care about the papers. There's something else. Only I don't know what it is."

"Wasn't it the prince, not DeLaBina, who sent you here?" asked Agrippa.

"That's true," admitted Fabrizio. "I didn't even say anything to him. I was just looking at him, hoping he would help me."

"Maybe he wanted to get you out of that room."

"He could have asked me to go," said Fabrizio. "I'd have been happy to leave."

"Ah! But the dead can't proclaim their innocence, can they?"

"Does that mean you won't kill me?" asked Fabrizio.

The executioner shook his head. "God made men. Men make laws. Isn't that what life is all about?"

"Or death," Fabrizio felt obliged to say. "But you don't seem to understand: If something happens to me, things will go badly for my master. I'm supposed to protect him, and he's about to be arrested."

"The magician?"

Fabrizio nodded, leaned back, and closed his eyes.

Agrippa leaned forward and tapped the boy on his leg. "Tell me, by any chance, did that master of yours teach you some magic?"

"I was just learning," said Fabrizio.

"It's a start."

Suddenly, Fabrizio said, "I really shouldn't — my master would not be pleased — but I could show you some magic . . . for an extra hour of life."

"I could do that," said Agrippa.

Remembering what Mangus had done at his performance, Fabrizio rolled back the sleeves of his tunic to show nothing was hidden. He showed the backs of his hands. He extended his right hand to show it empty, too. With a quick wave of his left hand, he made it appear as if a few coins dropped out of Agrippa's nose.

"Bravo!" said the executioner with grinning delight. "Milking people's noses for coins. A lovely way to become rich! Show me some more."

"Another hour?" asked Fabrizio.

"Agreed."

Fabrizio, recalling the images in Mangus's magic book, showed an empty hand, before making some coins appear and disappear.

"Wonderful!" said Agrippa. "If I didn't know otherwise, I'd say you had a great future. Why don't you teach me? An excellent way for me to entertain my guests."

"If I did, would you let me escape?"

"Can't."

"What about four more hours?" countered Fabrizio.

"That would give you" — Agrippa counted on his big

92

fingers — "an extra six hours to live. Just realize that in the end, it all comes to the same thing."

"Fine." Fabrizio was just about to turn one coin into another when a loud knocking burst upon the door.

"Boy!" cried the executioner. "Prepare yourself for death!" As he opened the door, Fabrizio fell to his knees and began to murmur frantic prayers.

# CHAPTER 10

STANDING ON THE THRESHOLD WAS A COURTIER WHOSE bright clothing appeared like a bonfire in the dungeon's foul gloom. One hand bore a lit lamp; the other hand held up a scroll.

"Signor Executioner, I bring a message from my lord."

Agrippa sighed. "I suppose I'm to break this clever boy's neck right away."

Fabrizio clapped his hands to his ears.

The courtier held out the paper. "Signore! It's not for me, a mere courtier, to read my lord's words. This message is solely for you." He handed the scroll to Agrippa, saluted, turned on his heels, and marched into the darkness.

Fabrizio, heart beating to burst, remained crouched in a corner and watched Agrippa through tear-blurred eyes.

With clumsy care, the executioner unrolled the scroll and gazed at what was written.

Fabrizio fell to his knees. "If you spare me!" he croaked. "I'll teach you all the magic I know!"

The executioner continued to stare at the scroll. "To tell the truth," he said, looking up. "I'm uncertain what to do. I don't know how to read."

"Signore," said Fabrizio with a surge of hope, "begging your pardon, but with permission, I read . . . a little."

Agrippa brightened. "Do you? What a clever lad! Reading has always seemed like magic to me. And you're a magician's servant. By all means, be so kind as to tell me what's written here." He held out the scroll.

Fabrizio reached for it.

Agrippa pulled it back abruptly. "One moment, Signore! I've no doubt this paper commands me to kill you instantly. But I need to be sure. I want your sacred promise that you'll tell me exactly what's written here."

"My master told me to always speak the truth."

"A good man. Still, are *you* prepared to swear by all that's good, clean, and holy that you'll be honest?"

"Cross my heart and hope to die, Signore."

"Well said! If more people held such hopes, my work would be less." He offered the scroll to Fabrizio. "Go on."

Wondering if he would be able to read the writing, Fabrizio took the scroll into his shaking hands. The light in the room being murky, he moved to the glowing coals, knelt down, and held the paper to the light. Resisting the desire to burn it, he gazed upon the paper. The letters seemed to dance before his eyes.

"Well," said Agrippa, "what does it say?"

Heart pounding, Fabrizio attempted to make sense of the scrawled hand, trying, as it were, to lift the letters, sound them, make sense of them. Gradually, he pieced together the words he thought he knew.

*Let . . . the boy . . .*

Unfortunately, these words were followed by a word he absolutely did *not* know. But at the end came . . . *d* —

Fabrizio sounded the first letter under his breath, then the next letter, and the next . . .

His heart lurched. It was the same word he had unraveled that morning during his reading lesson: *Death!* That's what the word said! *Death.*

Horrified, he tried to make sense of the fourth word by putting its sounds together. The more he went over them, the queasier he became. In the end, he decided it didn't matter what that fourth word said: The order demanded his immediate death.

But who'd sent it? Fabrizio scrutinized the part of the writing that was — he assumed — the signature: a single, scrawled letter.

As he thought about it, he decided that the only one who could make things worse was the king. And indeed, the courtier said it was "my lord" who had sent it. That made sense to Fabrizio when he recalled how fearful the king was. Therefore, the letter used to sign the paper was *C* for Claudio.

"Come now," Agrippa said with increasing impatience. "What does the order say?"

Tense, Fabrizio closed his eyes.

"Boy!" growled Agrippa. "You promised to read what is truly written here."

Fabrizio, almost whispering, said, "Signore . . . It says . . . it says . . . 'Let the boy . . . go . . . free!'"

"Does it? Perfectly amazing! In all my years that's never happened before." Suddenly, Agrippa frowned. "Do you swear solemnly it says that exactly?"

"It does, Signore." Fabrizio avoided Agrippa's eyes. " 'Let the boy go free.' Yes. That's what it says."

"Who signed it?"

Fabrizio steadied himself. "*C* for Claudio."

*"The king?"* cried an amazed Agrippa. "Claudio?"

"You're welcome to look." Fabrizio offered the scroll to the executioner.

Agrippa took the paper into his dirty hands and examined it with his blinking eyes. "I suppose there's a first time for everything. I'm glad because I've taken a liking to you. The king himself, you say."

"The king, Signore," whispered Fabrizio. "No doubt."

"Bless him for a kindly fellow. I'm honored he wrote me. Signor Fabrizio, the door is now open to you. You can go. Just know that if you are ever sent back here to be executed, you'll find in me a friend who will kill you with great affection and consideration."

"Signore," said Fabrizio, feeling guilty for saving his own life, "if I must die, I can think of no one better than you to do your duty. But, with permission, I think I'll leave right away."

"I'd tell you the way to the street. But I've been here so long I no longer know the way. Just offer that paper to anyone you meet. Since King Claudio himself says you're free to go, you'll be shown the way."

The executioner held out a large hand in friendship. Fabrizio shook it. "I'm proud to shake your hand."

"For my part, Signor Agrippa," said Fabrizio, "I'm glad your hand is shaking my hand and not my neck. Many, many thanks."

With that, Fabrizio walked out of the executioner's cell and hurried down the narrow passageway. At the first bend, he paused and looked back. Agrippa was at the doorway, waving a friendly good-bye. Fabrizio did the same, and turned the corner. No sooner did he do so than he found himself in complete darkness with no idea where to go.

# CHAPTER 11

$\mathcal{T}$HE MORE FABRIZIO STOOD IN THE DARKNESS, THE MORE panicky he became. He must get home and warn Mangus of his imminent arrest. But which way should he go?

Realizing he was still clutching the execution paper, he tossed it in one direction and started off the opposite way. Though he moved cautiously, he tripped and came crashing down.

Dizzy, he forced himself up and extended his hands to center himself, then resumed walking with greater caution. When he next bumped into something, he felt around him and discovered that he had found steps leading up. Since he had originally come *down*, going *up* seemed the right thing to do.

Moments later, he reached — or so he guessed, for it was still dark — a landing. He pushed on.

A glimmer of light appeared ahead. Fabrizio was soon able to make out the contours of a hallway. He stepped around a bend and came into a deserted passageway lit by a candle lantern that hung from the ceiling. At the far end were more steps.

He bounded up, then hurried along another hallway until he came to walls made of smoother stones, and, then, a wooden door.

He put an ear against it. Quiet. The door handle would not turn. The keyhole revealed nothing.

Fabrizio hurried on. More doors appeared and by every door hung a large key. He took one down and fitted it into the nearest door's keyhole. He eased open the door.

Inside was a small room with a narrow bed. Walls and floor and ceiling were stone. A thin blanket had been tossed onto the foot of the bed. A small, high window with rusty bars let in a little light.

He decided he had come upon a row of prison cells. The realization made him shut the door, replace the key, and run around a bend only to hear voices ahead. Reversing himself, he scampered back and listened.

"In you go!" The loud cry was followed by a slamming door, diminishing steps, and then silence.

Fabrizio peered around the bend. Seeing no one, he stepped into the corridor and scrutinized the doors. Someone must have been locked inside a cell. But which one?

He pressed his ear to one of the doors. *Silence.* He checked the next, and the next. It was behind the fifth door that he heard a small sound from inside. Someone was moving around. *An unfortunate prisoner,* he thought. Maybe he'll know of a way to escape.

Fabrizio was still trying to decide what to do when he heard more voices. Alarmed, he shoved the key into the lock, pushed open the door, and slipped inside the cell, taking the key with him.

In the weak light he saw a man upon the narrow bed, face turned toward the rough wall. A tattered blanket covered him. The more Fabrizio gazed at the prisoner, the more the man's stillness suggested he might be dead. He stepped forward to get a better look, but then heard voices from the hallway again.

Frantic, Fabrizio shoved the door shut, only to realize that he had just trapped himself inside the cell.

# CHAPTER 12

A PANICKY FABRIZIO LOOKED AROUND. THERE WAS ONLY one place to hide: beneath the bed. Flopping onto his belly, he squeezed under it and then yanked the old blanket down. For once, he was grateful for his small size.

"What happened to the key?" someone barked from right outside the door. Fabrizio's heart jumped. He knew the voice: Primo Magistrato DeLaBina.

"I have no idea, Signore," came the reply.

Fabrizio tried to make himself smaller. If DeLaBina discovered him, he surely would be sent back to the executioner and put immediately to death.

"The door's open, Magistrato."

"Open? He must have been able to get to the key and flee. Hurry, look inside!"

Fabrizio tugged down the tattered blanket even more. He was able to peek through a small hole in time to see the cell door open. A pair of rough soldier's boots entered. Another pair, much finer, came right after. Lantern light fell upon the floor.

"He's still here, Signor Magistrato."

"Are you sure it's him?"

The not-so-fine boots approached. Fabrizio held his breath.

"It's him, Signore."

"He looks dead. Hold up your lamp."

"Asleep."

"Where's the key?"

Fabrizio shoved the key against the wall and pressed himself flatter against the cold floor.

"I don't see it, Magistrato."

"Wake him and make him tell us where he put it."

The bed shook over Fabrizio. "Here, you, Signore! Wake up!"

"What . . . is it?"

Fabrizio was so startled by the drowsy voice that he pushed a hand against his mouth to keep from crying out.

"Mangus!" shouted DeLaBina. "What did you do with the key?"

"The key . . . ? With the greatest respect, Signore, I . . .

I don't know what you are talking about. I've . . . I've been asleep."

"Don't fool with me, Mangus. You were locked in this room. The key was outside. How did you get it?"

Mangus sighed. "Signore, if I had the key, why would I remain in this awful place? Be reasonable."

"I'm not interested in reason!" bellowed DeLaBina. "What magic did you use to get that key?"

"I don't do magic," said Mangus.

"Get him up," said DeLaBina. "We'll put him in another cell, and this time take the key with us. No, wait! I've been informed he uses his hands to work his magic. Another cell would be useless. Do you have some rope?"

"Yes, Signore."

"Good. Tie his hands to either side of the bed."

Fabrizio clenched his teeth in anger.

"Signor Magistrato," pleaded Mangus. "I beg mercy."

"You'll have some mercy when you reveal who asked you to make the papers."

"It's no different from what I told you when you first

came to me: I didn't make the papers, and I don't know who did."

"Signor Mangus, if you don't cooperate, you'll suffer the same fate as your servant boy."

Fabrizio lifted his head off the floor.

"What do you mean?" asked Mangus. "What's happened to him?"

"Prince Cosimo had him executed."

"Executed! God have mercy! The boy may be an ignorant scamp, but I can't believe he did anything to deserve death. Why should the prince have done such a thing?"

"Your boy was interfering, that's why. Now, Signor Mangus, listen to me carefully. I am prepared to do what's necessary to get you to confess that it was Count Scarazoni who told you to make those papers."

"Scarazoni? Signore, I have never even met the count."

"Pay heed, Mangus! Unless you admit that it's Scarazoni who is trying to depose the king, you'll suffer the same fate as your boy."

"But, Signore, I know nothing about what the count does or does not do."

"Signor Mangus," said DeLaBina, "must I remind you that magic is illegal in Pergamontio? The penalty is death. I am the primo magistrato. Cooperate with me. I can help you. Now, is he tied down?"

"Yes, Magistrato."

"Mangus, I must meet someone. When I return, I'll expect you to confess the truth about Scarazoni."

The door slammed shut.

## CHAPTER 13

**F**ABRIZIO LISTENED TO THE SOUND OF RETREATING STEPS. When he was sure the magistrato had truly gone, he scrambled out. "Master, I'm here. As alive as you!"

Mangus twisted his head around. "Fabrizio! They told me you were executed."

"As it's said, 'Believe your own eyes before you believe the mouth of your neighbors.'"

"I would hardly describe DeLaBina as my neighbor," growled Mangus. "Where did you come from?"

"Under the bed, Master. Let me untie you!"

"Was it you who took the cell key?" asked Mangus as Fabrizio worked to loosen the ropes.

A grinning Fabrizio held it up.

Mangus shook his head. "I don't know whether to scold or applaud you."

"I'm just trying to help, Master."

Mangus, sitting on the edge of the bed while rubbing his wrists where the ropes had bound him, said nothing.

"Master, you look poorly."

"I've not been treated with kindness. Now, how did you get here?"

"It's a long story, Master."

"I suppose I must hear. But lock the door. Hopefully, that self-important fool won't be back soon."

Fabrizio did as he was told and sat on the floor before his master. Then he related everything, from the time he went from the house to his leaving the executioner. When he was finished, Mangus remained silent and frowning.

"Have I done something wrong, Master?"

"Did I not tell you to do nothing that might cast suspicion on me?"

"Master, I thought I was doing what you asked."

"I did not have this result in mind," said Mangus.

Upset, Fabrizio asked, "With permission, Master, how did you get here?"

"After DeLaBina caught you spreading the papers around the city —"

"Master, I was *collecting* them!"

"— he came to the house, accused me of telling you to distribute those papers, and then arrested me."

"Master," said Fabrizio, "I heard DeLaBina say he wanted you to confess that it was Count Scarazoni who asked you to make the papers."

"True," said Mangus, "but of course the count told me no such thing." He paused to think. "I had heard that the prince and the count are rivals, but what you observed during your meeting with the king suggests the count and the magistrato are also at odds."

"It was as if they were dueling," agreed Fabrizio.

"Did DeLaBina accuse Count Scarazoni?"

"No, Master. But there were lots of daggers in that room — even the king had one. They all looked ready to use them."

"Though DeLaBina has accused and threatened me," Mangus mused, "it does seem that the one he's really after is Scarazoni."

"Is that possible, Master?"

"It was the Greek philosopher Heraclitus who said, 'If we do not expect the unexpected, we will never find it.'

Fabrizio, I suppose you heard DeLaBina suggest he would not punish me if I named the count as the traitor."

"I know you won't lie, Master."

Mangus retreated into his own thoughts, then said, "Fabrizio, the message that came to the executioner, the one that ordered your *immediate* death. Tell me about it."

"Master, I read it."

"*Read* it, Fabrizio?"

Fabrizio put a hand to his heart. "I absolutely read the word *death*. You'll be pleased I knew it because of that writing by your friend, Signor Dante. The message said, 'Let the boy . . .' After that came a word I didn't know. But it was followed by the word — I'm sure of it — *death*."

"Fabrizio, to miss one word in a sentence is like missing the pearl in the oyster. It may still be edible, but it's not valuable. Show me the paper."

"Forgive me, Master," said Fabrizio. "I feared it would be found on me and then I'd be executed. I threw it away."

Mangus sighed. "Did anyone sign it?"

"Absolutely, Master. I read it. A single letter . . . a *C*. I think."

"*Think* or *know*?"

"Wouldn't the . . . *C* fit King Claudio?"

"Yes!" said Mangus angrily. "Or Prince Cosimo. But if an *S*, Scarazoni. Or a *D*, DeLaBina! Fabrizio, the fact is, you really don't know what you read. Because you can't read! And that means you've no idea who wished to execute you quickly!"

"Master, I tried."

"The way you tried to collect the papers and brought us here?"

Fabrizio hung his head. After a time, he said, "Master, I just remembered something else. Scarazoni knew of you."

"Too many people know me," grumbled Mangus. "The question remains, what is DeLaBina trying to do? Is he truly after Scarazoni? And if so, why?"

"Master," offered Fabrizio, "I can tell you something else."

Mangus looked at the boy bleakly.

"When the magistrato arrested me, guess who was standing by on the street watching and . . . smiling? Giuseppe."

"Giuseppe! Good heaven! What are you suggesting? Giuseppe knows nothing about this business."

Fabrizio blushed. "Forgive me, Master, but Benito and Giuseppe forced me to reveal what DeLaBina said when he came to the house. They even said they know people who would like to know about this matter. And, Master . . . I heard the magistrato say . . . he had . . . an informant."

Mangus's face turned red with anger. "How dare you! For years Benito and Giuseppe have been my loyal servants! DeLaBina has many informants. Why should I even bother talking to you about this? You cause nothing but trouble. Now, be still! I must think!"

Crushed, Fabrizio obeyed. But after a few minutes he blurted out, "Master, have you figured out how those papers came to be so alike?"

"Of course not!"

"Forgive me, Master, I may be ignorant, but it still seems to me as if a devil is mixing and confusing things to make your life miserable."

"Fabrizio, philosophy teaches that when seeking an

answer one must look for the *simplest* explanation. *You* keep complicating matters!"

"But . . ."

"Be still! The truth is you've made a muddle of everything!"

Fabrizio shrank down. Wishing Mistress Sophia were there, he recalled her words: "Take care of him . . . prove how useful you can be."

"Master," said Fabrizio, "don't you think it would be best if we escaped from this place?"

"How do you expect me to do that?" snapped Mangus.

Fabrizio pointed to the key in the door.

"Where would I go?"

"I've many street friends, Master. They would hide you. There's an excellent place right below the fish market. It doesn't smell too badly. Or, what about Signor Galda of the Sign of the Crown? He cares for you."

"DeLaBina would find me quickly and matters would become even worse."

Fabrizio stood up. "With permission, Master. I'm going to search for a way out."

"Good. I could use some quiet to ponder all of this."

"I'll not be long." Fabrizio started for the door.

"Fabrizio!"

"Yes, Master?"

"Fabrizio . . . I think it best if you did not return. It's quite clear there is . . . no future for you with me. I'm not sure if I even have a future. Just . . . go off. On your own. I don't want you around anymore."

Stunned, Fabrizio turned around. "Master, are you . . . are you . . . dismissing me from your service?"

"I can't afford to be entangled by your ignorance anymore. I have troubles enough."

"But, Master," pleaded Fabrizio, "as they say, 'If you buy a dog, you also get his fleas.'"

"When I want a dog, I'll buy a dog! It's best you leave my service. Go!" With that, Mangus rolled over on the bed.

It was all Fabrizio could do to keep from bursting into tears. "Master . . . please, I —"

"Leave!" cried Mangus.

"Yes, Master. With permission, forgive . . . me."

Hardly knowing what to do, Fabrizio fumbled with the key and opened the door. At the threshold he paused. "A thousand, million thanks, Master. Farewell. And . . . please say . . . good-bye to Mistress."

Mangus neither moved nor spoke.

"What shall I do with the key?" Fabrizio whispered.

"Put it where you found it."

Choked and tearful, Fabrizio stepped into the hallway and slowly shut the door behind him. Though the corridor was cold and empty, he felt hot and heavy. A sob clogged his throat. He'd failed. He was homeless once more. And now he'd never see Mistress again.

Pressing his forehead against the stone wall, he began to cry. His shoulders shook. Gradually, his crying subsided. He pushed his hair from his face and smeared away the tears with the back of his hand. The corridor appeared as bleak as he felt. Wanting to fulfill Mangus's last request, Fabrizio returned the key to its peg and forced himself to step away. After a few paces he stopped and looked back.

His tear-blurred eyes made the doors all look alike. He was no longer certain which cell was Mangus's.

"It doesn't matter," Fabrizio muttered. He took the lantern down from the wall and started to walk away.

Suddenly, he heard, "Find the magician's cell!"

Alarmed, Fabrizio grabbed the nearest key and unlocked the closest door, then shut it behind him.

The room was identical to the one in which Mangus lay, even to its narrow bed and small, high window. To Fabrizio's surprise, however, some of the treasonous papers were scattered about on the floor. Moreover, sitting on the bed was a small and huddled humanlike creature, wearing trousers, a long shirt, and boots.

As Fabrizio stared, a blackened face surrounded by long red hair, with eyes that smoldered with anger, glared back at him fiercely.

Fabrizio stammered, "What . . . what are you?"

"The devil."

# CHAPTER 14

FABRIZIO'S BODY TURNED COLD. BARELY ABLE TO BREATHE, he threw himself against the cell door and stared wide-eyed.

"Who are *you*?" the creature demanded.

"A . . . a . . . boy."

"What do you want?"

Behind his back, Fabrizio fumbled frantically for the door handle. "I . . . I was passing by."

"Passing by?" returned a voice full of mockery. "In a prison? The door was locked. How did you get in? Did you bring some food? Water?"

All Fabrizio could say was, "Are you truly . . . actually . . . the . . . devil?"

"That's what I'm called," came the proud answer.

"What . . . else might you be called?" asked Fabrizio.

"My name, stupid!"

"What . . . what's your name?"

"Maria!" the creature all but shouted.

"But . . . but Maria is a holy saint's name. And a girl's name at that."

"Why shouldn't I be called Maria? I *am* a girl."

"A *female* devil?" said Fabrizio. "I never heard of anything like that. But you . . . you don't dress like a girl."

"These" — Maria gestured to her clothing — "are my working clothes. Do you have objections to girls who work?"

"Oh, no, Signorina," said Fabrizio, unable to take his eyes from Maria's sooty face. "But, didn't you say you were the . . . devil?"

"You didn't ask my *name*," said the girl. "You asked me what I *was*."

"Signorina, with the most deep and profound apologies. You must forgive me. I never met a devil before."

"This whole city is full of stupid devils."

"It is?" cried Fabrizio.

"There I was walking down the street, when I was arrested for doing my business."

"With permission, Signorina Devil, what is your business?"

"Passing these papers around." Maria gestured to the ones on the ground.

"You . . . were? When?"

"Yesterday. And I've been here ever since."

Fabrizio put up his hands in protest. "But, Signorina Maria Devil, where did you get them?"

"I helped make them."

"*Make* them?" whispered Fabrizio, in shock.

"Every time I say something, you come back like a stupid echo. Do you have a name?"

"Fabrizio."

"And *you*, Signor Fabrizio, are *you* a devil?"

"Oh, no, no, not at all," he assured her, hastily making the sign of the cross over his heart. "But, Signorina Maria Devil, please, did you use magic to make these papers?"

"Magic? It took hard work, paper, and ink."

"*Ink?*"

"What do you think I'm covered with?"

"Signorina Devil, I —"

"Stop calling me 'devil'! If you don't call me Maria, I won't talk to you."

"Yes, of course. Maria Devil, then. But why was the work hard?"

"I suppose you think it's easy to use a printing press."

Fabrizio stared blankly at the girl. "What's a . . . a . . . pant . . . presser?"

"A . . . *printing* . . . press!" said the girl with loud, overstated slowness, as if Fabrizio were hard of hearing.

"Forgive me, Signorina. In my whole entire life I've never heard of such a . . . thing."

"That's because you live in the most ignorant, backward city in all of Italy. Printing is our *work*. My parents —"

"Are *they* devils, too?" asked Fabrizio.

"*I'm* the printer's devil!" Maria cried, slapping herself on her chest.

A baffled Fabrizio sat on the bed as far away from the girl as possible. "Signorina, I beg you — tell me about this . . . pressed . . . painting."

Exasperated, Maria leaned back against the stone wall and closed her eyes. "I'm tired of answering stupid questions. Just try to understand. We — that's to say my parents and I — came from Milan. We brought along the German invention, *the printing press*. Though the invention is forty years old, and lots of places in Italy have one, this kingdom is such a backward, *stupid* place it has no printing press. It may be 1490, but you all dress, talk, act, and think as if it were still the Dark Ages."

"Signorina —"

"Don't interrupt. We came here to start a printing business. Fine! My parents purchased a license from the authorities and put the press together."

"Is it a . . . machine?"

"You could call it that. Mostly, my task is to rub the ink on the letters, help with the printing, clean the type, and put it away."

"Can you read?" asked Fabrizio.

"Lord of heaven! Of course I can read. Can't you?"

"Not really."

Maria rolled her eyes. "Pergamontio is the most ignorant place!"

"Signorina, I beg you, go on with your story."

"Fine. I usually deliver what we print. So, after we printed these papers — some four hundred of them — I was told to pass them about the city. I had almost finished when I was arrested.

"The work I do keeps me filthy most of the time. That's why I'm called a 'printer's devil.' I'm filthy because the ink I work with is hard to scrub off. Now do you understand?"

"I'm trying to," said Fabrizio. "But this . . . machine, this . . . presser."

Maria grunted with frustration. "Printing press. Do you know how writing gets onto paper?"

Fabrizio, recalling what Mangus had told him, brightened. "Each letter is written out by hand. It takes forever. At a scriptorium."

"That's the old-fashioned way. The German invention — the printing press — *imitates* writing to perfection. It's cheaper, faster, and makes each page look exactly like the other."

*"Exactly?"* cried Fabrizio, excited by this revelation.

"It's as my mother says: 'The inked type kisses the paper so wonderfully the paper never forgets.'"

Fabrizio jumped off the bed. "Signorina, are you truly telling me that the way these papers" — he gestured to the floor — "came to be *exactly* the same as the others is by your . . . printing machine?"

"Why else do you think Signor Gutenberg invented it?"

"Because he's the devil?"

"No! *I* am the printer's devil, but by the name of God, I assure you, our work has nothing to do with devils."

"Good!" Fabrizio clapped his hands with glee. "You've told me more than you know. The mystery of the many same papers is solved! I'll tell my master. He'll be thrilled. Where is this machine?"

"At my house."

"I'd love to see it. And so will my master. But, Signorina, another very important question. Was it your parents' idea to make —?"

"Print," the girl corrected.

"To . . . *print* those papers?"

"You are so stupid! I told you: My parents were just setting up the business. By the time we got here, we had no more money. With someone willing to pay them to do the job, they were not going to turn it down. In fact, after they got their printing license, it was their first work in Pergamontio."

"Well then," said an excited Fabrizio, "who asked them to do the job?"

"I have no idea, though I did wonder who might be trying to overthrow your king."

"Was it your parents?"

Maria pulled away. "You don't listen well. Somebody *told* my parents what to print. A printer's job is to make words appear. It's censors who make them disappear. Printers fight censors all the time. I hate censors!" She crossed her arms. "I still don't understand who you are and why you're even here."

"Signorina, as I said, my name is Fabrizio, and I'm trying to do a huge number of things. Number one: Protect my master who sits in a cell down the hall. I have failed completely. Two: Get rid of these treasonous papers.

Failed again, miserably. Three: Find out how the papers were made. Which — *brava!* — you have explained. Four: Find the one who ordered the papers. Five: Tell DeLaBina. When I do all that, my master will be free and, without doubt, he'll let me live in his house forever, which will make me the happiest boy in the whole entire city."

Maria shrugged. "The only person I know in this stupid place is the fellow who arrested me. I don't even know his name. But he's fat, sweats a lot, and is pompous."

"That's DeLaBina! The primo magistrato. The chief prosecutor, in charge of all laws and licenses. A great power here in Pergamontio. Amazing! He arrested you, me, and my master."

"Why were you arrested?"

"For the same reason as you: putting these papers around the city."

"But you didn't. It was me."

"True! I was trying to get rid of them — to help my master. Still, when I got here, Prince Cosimo sent me to be executed. But I was clever enough to get free."

"You're still in prison. That's not very free."

"I was on my way out."

"I'd like to get out, too," said Maria.

"So would my master. I just wish you had told DeLaBina about your printing machine."

"He already knew," said Maria.

"He did?" cried Fabrizio. He thought for a moment. "Of course! He's in charge of all licenses. Your parents must have gotten theirs from *him*."

"Maybe."

"If they did, it means DeLaBina was lying to my master!" Fabrizio related how DeLaBina accused Mangus of making the papers.

"Are you suggesting," said Maria, "it was DeLaBina who asked my parents to make them?"

Fabrizio nodded. "But that didn't keep him from charging my master with using magic to make them!" Fabrizio jumped up and went to the door of the cell. "I must tell my master about your machine and that DeLaBina knew all along that it was your parents who made the papers."

Maria slumped back against the wall. "I wish I knew where my parents are."

Fabrizio swung around. "What do you mean?"

Tears filled Maria's eyes. "They've disappeared. I'm really worried about them. Wouldn't you be if your parents were gone?"

"Forgive me, my parents died some time ago."

Maria bobbed her head. "I'm sorry."

"Did DeLaBina know anything about your parents' whereabouts?"

Maria shook her head. "That was the one thing he didn't know. In fact, he said he must find them. He kept questioning me as to where they might be."

"Don't you have any idea?"

Maria shook her head.

"I'm sure my master could help."

"How?"

"My master knows more about things appearing and disappearing than anyone in the whole world. He's a magician."

Maria sniffed. "There's no such thing as magic."

"Of course there is. And he's taught me. Look."

Fabrizio reached into his pocket, pulled out his hand, and made some motions so that it appeared as if a coin came from her nose. "There," he said. "Magic."

"You took the coin from your pocket, hid it in your palm, and then slipped it into your other hand," said Maria.

Fabrizio sighed. "I need more practice."

"Do you live with this magician?" asked Maria.

"I did. He just dismissed me because . . . of this business with DeLaBina. But when I tell him how those papers were made, I'm sure he'll be so happy he'll take me back. So, with permission, Signorina Devil, I'll go to him." He got up and put his ear to the cell door and listened. Hearing nothing, he poked his head out. No one was in the hallway.

"I'm going," he whispered over his shoulder.

Maria jumped up. "I'm coming with you."

"Good. You can tell him about your machine."

As Fabrizio stepped into the hallway, Maria picked up the lantern and followed.

After locking the cell door behind them, Fabrizio hung the key in its proper place. Next he gazed up and down the corridor, hoping he'd recognize which door led to Mangus.

"I thought you said he was right here."

"He is," Fabrizio insisted, trying desperately to remember the right door. "Somewhere."

Maria leaned against the wall, arms folded over her chest. "Why don't you use magic?" she suggested.

Embarrassed, Fabrizio said, "I'm sure it's this door. Master!" he called into the door crack.

There was no reply.

He went on to the next door and called. Again no reply. A glance at Maria convinced him she was looking at him with scorn.

He pulled down a key, put it in the nearest lock, and turned. It opened.

"I've found him!" announced Fabrizio as he poked his head inside.

But the cell was empty.

## CHAPTER 15

FABRIZIO, PRAYING HE HAD GONE INTO THE WRONG CELL, went to the bed, dropped to his knees, and gathered up the blanket that lay there. He examined its edge. "A hole," he announced, his heart sinking.

"There are always holes in blankets," said Maria impatiently.

"When I was hiding under my master's bed I peeked out through this *exact* hole. I'm sure of it."

"Why were you hiding under your master's bed?"

"I can't explain now. But right after I left him I heard voices. Someone was coming for him. I jumped into your cell so no one would catch me. I didn't know who it was, but if it was DeLaBina, I just pray he didn't send Master to be executed. He threatened to."

"Fabrizio," said Maria, "I'm truly sorry for your troubles. And for your master's. But I have to find my parents." She took a step away.

Fabrizio, thinking about what might have happened to Mangus, didn't move.

The girl pulled on his sleeve. "Once we're free and I find my parents, I'll help you look for your master." She held the lamp before her and set off through the hallways. Her red hair seemed to smolder.

After a moment, a pensive Fabrizio followed, passing through one deserted hallway after another. From what seemed like far away, the cathedral bells began to toll. The two halted and counted out the twelve peals.

"Midnight," said Maria and started up again with Fabrizio by her side.

Yelling shattered the silence: "What are you doing here? We were supposed to meet elsewhere."

Fabrizio and Maria stopped immediately.

"I think . . . I think that's DeLaBina!" Fabrizio whispered.

"You've acted like a fool," returned another voice. "That magician believes you're the one behind all the papers and what we're doing."

"What makes you so sure?"

"I spoke to him in his cell."

"Don't worry. I have him under control."

"And those papers?"

"They were made on something called a printing press."

"How do you know?"

"I arranged it."

"You! I thought it was the magician. Why didn't you tell me? We'll be found out!"

"Not a chance! We're making progress. You're such a fool! Just because you —"

A horrible scream erupted.

Fabrizio and Maria spun around and ran as fast as they could. After a few minutes they stopped to catch their breath. "What happened?" Maria whispered. "Who was the other person?"

"I wish I knew," said Fabrizio, gulping for air.

"Fabrizio, we need to get out of here." Walking fast, she led the way through one dismal hallway after another. It was as if they were going in circles. Then, as they turned still another corner, Fabrizio gasped. He grabbed the lantern from Maria and held it high.

"Look!"

On the ground, a large body covered by a black robe lay still. The head was covered but the legs stuck out.

"Is he . . . alive?" Maria whispered.

Fabrizio edged forward and knelt down. Then he reached out and drew back the robe. Beneath lay a man with his head twisted to one side. A ruby-encrusted dagger was sticking out of his back. On the ground a pool of wet blood was spreading.

"That's . . . that's the man who arrested me," a shocked Maria stammered.

"It's DeLaBina. That must have been him screaming. And . . ." whispered Fabrizio, "I recognize that dagger. It's the king's."

Grabbing Maria's hand, he pulled her along the hallway as fast as he could. But barely did they turn the first corner when they all but ran into someone. Jumping back, Fabrizio held up the lantern.

It was somebody wearing a long black robe.

"Blessed God!" cried Fabrizio. He turned, prepared to flee, only to bump into Maria.

"Stand where you are!" the black-robed figure shouted

from behind the hood that hid his face. His voice was so commanding that Fabrizio and Maria felt compelled to obey.

"What are you doing here?" demanded the black robe.

Not knowing what else to do, Fabrizio bowed. "Signore, I'm just a servant." Then, remembering Mangus's words, "Pay attention to what's visible and you can discover what's hidden," he scrutinized the figure. But the man was so wrapped around within his black robe, from the tip of one red boot to the top of his hidden head, Fabrizio could not begin to guess who it might be.

"Why," demanded the black robe, "are you wandering around here?"

"Forgive us . . . Signore," said Maria. "We . . . we . . . wanted to visit a prisoner. But we couldn't find him, so we were trying to leave. And go home. We've become lost. Perhaps, Signore, you can tell us the way out."

As if pondering Maria's request, the black robe remained motionless. "Who were you trying to visit?" he finally asked.

"Mangus the Magician," said Fabrizio. "I . . . I used to be his servant."

"Were you not to be executed?" said the black robe.

"Signore, the . . . king freed me."

"The king! Why?"

"I have no idea," said Fabrizio.

The black robe made no response. Fabrizio could not tell if the man was even looking at him.

"Forgive me, Signore," Fabrizio ventured timidly. "Do you . . . know if Mangus was . . . executed?"

The black robe did not answer. Instead, he said, "Have you seen anyone else?"

"Signor DeLaBina," said Maria.

The black robe turned to her sharply. "Where?"

"Back there." Maria pointed in the direction where they had discovered the body. "Not far."

"Did you . . . did you speak to him?"

"Signore," said Maria, "the dead can't speak."

The black robe grew still, as if trying to make up his mind. Next moment, he turned and walked in a direction opposite to where DeLaBina lay. After a few paces he stopped abruptly and turned. "The way out is in *that* direction." He pointed a white-gloved hand toward another corridor. "Continue along," said the black robe, pointing. "Make a left, then a right. You'll find a door. It's not locked. You may leave the building that way. Indeed, I urge you to leave the city." That said, the black robe turned and strode away in haste.

"Many thanks, Signore!" Fabrizio called. He and Maria stared after him until his footsteps became faint and he disappeared into the gloom.

"Come on!" cried Maria, and she ran down the corridor with Fabrizio close behind. When they reached the first turning, they paused.

"Fabrizio," said Maria, quite breathless, "do you have any . . . any idea who *that* . . . was?"

"He couldn't have been the king. When I told him the king freed me, he acted surprised."

"Who was it, then?"

"His voice sounded like the one we heard talking to DeLaBina before the scream. I'll tell you one thing: Count Scarazoni hated DeLaBina."

"Would this Scarazoni have murdered him?"

"He has a reputation for killing people."

"Why did he tell us to leave Pergamontio?" asked Maria.

"Everybody asks me to leave," said Fabrizio. "Come on."

They raced on. At the end of a passageway was a door. One hard shove and it swung open onto a rush of damp air and fog. They bolted out, but they could see almost nothing.

Although Maria was standing only a few feet away, she appeared as little more than a shadow.

"Fabrizio?" she called.

"Right here!"

She drew close. "Do you know where we are?"

"I suppose behind the Hall of Justice."

Straining to see through the swirling mist, they started walking. The fog began to thin. They could see a little.

"Stop!" whispered Fabrizio.

"What is it?"

"Look!"

A dark figure — some sixty paces away — seemed to float up out of the gloom.

"It's the black robe again!" said Fabrizio.

# CHAPTER 16

$\mathfrak{F}$ABRIZIO BACKED UP.

"Fabrizio," cried Maria, "there are two black robes!"

Sure enough, two figures, one tall, one short, both cloaked in black robes, loomed out of the eddying fog. One of the figures was about Mangus's height.

Fabrizio could not restrain himself. "Master!" he called. No reply came. The black robes vanished into the fog.

"Was that your master?" asked Maria, her voice hushed.

"I thought so, but I really don't know. Maria, I need to go to his house."

He gazed around, trying to get his bearings. "I'll take you home first. But we need to be careful. The curfew is still on. DeLaBina's soldiers are always on patrol. We're not supposed to be on the street."

"What if they see us?"

"We'd go back to prison."

"My house is on the Street of the Wood Sellers."

"Stay close!"

They hurried along, halting frequently to make sure they were not caught on the deserted streets. Once, they heard the tramp of footsteps. "The watch!" hissed Fabrizio. They hid behind some barrels.

"We'd better wait for a while," he suggested.

They settled back, keeping close for warmth and trying to be patient. Exhausted, at one point Fabrizio even dozed. So did Maria.

With a start, Fabrizio woke. The fog had thinned.

A faint glow to the east suggested dawn as the dark of night gave way to the iron blue of daylight. Cocks crowed. Pigeons fluttered. A dog barked and a hungry donkey brayed. As the cathedral bells tolled the hour, Fabrizio and Maria ran through the city's narrow, crooked streets, avoiding puddles of thin overnight ice. At every corner Fabrizio halted and surveyed what lay ahead.

"Your street is there," Fabrizio finally announced, pausing at yet another corner.

Maria poked her head around. With a start she pulled back.

"What's the matter?" asked Fabrizio.

"There's a soldier sitting in front of my house."

Fabrizio looked. A soldier dressed in a green court uniform was leaning against the front door of a small, flat-roofed, two-story house. Across his knees lay a sword.

"A king's soldier," said Fabrizio. "They aren't the usual night watch. Count Scarazoni controls them."

"Why would Scarazoni send a soldier to my house?"

"I don't know."

Fabrizio took a second look. "I think he's sleeping."

"We still won't be able to get in."

"Is there a back door?"

Maria nodded. They scampered down the street and around to the rear alley. The corner house had an old thick grapevine growing high against the wall. Pushing aside the brittle brown leaves, Maria and Fabrizio looked into the dirt alleyway.

It wasn't hard to pick out Maria's house. Another soldier was posted against a faded blue back door. He sat with legs stretched before him and a sword in easy reach.

Fabrizio gazed at him. "I have an idea," he said. "If I went along the alley and yelled something to get that soldier to chase me, you could race into the house. Are you fast?" he asked.

"Fast enough," said Maria. "But if he catches you, does that mean you'll go back to prison?"

"Don't worry. I can get past him. Then I'll circle back around and slip in. If I can't, I'll wait for you here. For a while, anyway. You're the one who has to get by him. You know what they say: A first chance is worth fifty second ones."

Maria, her face solemn, nodded.

"All right," said Fabrizio. "Here I go."

"Fabrizio . . ."

"What?"

Maria gave him a hug. "You're the only one in this whole city I like."

"Even though I'm stupid?"

She grinned. "I was wrong. You're smart."

Fabrizio stepped out from around the corner, took a quick look back at Maria, and ambled down the alley. Acting as if there were nothing in his mind, he kept his eyes fixed on the soldier.

As Fabrizio drew closer, the soldier shifted his head slightly.

*He's pretending to be asleep,* thought Fabrizio. *Good.*

When he came within thirty feet of the soldier, he saw the man's hand move stealthily toward the hilt of his sword.

Fabrizio ran past the soldier yelling, "Asleep! Asleep on duty!"

The soldier bolted up and groped for his sword. Trying to do both things made his movement awkward. "Halt!" he shouted. "In the name of the king! Halt!" He staggered after Fabrizio.

Fabrizio reached the alley's end. "Asleep! Asleep!" he jeered. He tore around the corner, plunged into the first recessed doorway, and pressed himself flat.

Moments later the soldier clumped by, yelling, "Halt! Halt!"

As soon as he passed, Fabrizio sprang from his hiding place and ran back to the faded blue door. He shoved it open, leaped inside, and slammed the door shut behind him. Where was Maria?

# CHAPTER 17

𝔄 LITTLE LIGHT SEEPED THROUGH THE SHUTTERED window, enough to allow Fabrizio to see that he was standing in a small room. Save for a pair of old and broken leather boots that lay upon the rough wooden floor, it was empty. He heard nothing. With care, he crept into a larger, darker room. It was heaped with household goods: pots, clothing, and a collapsed chair. Shreds of paper lay strewn about like feathers from a broken bed. On one paper, Fabrizio saw a bit of the treasonous message. Its letters were smeared.

"Maria?" he called softly.

Hearing a slight wheezing noise, he stepped into the next room. Maria was leaning back against the far wall, arms tight around her stomach. She was shaking. Tears slid down her inky cheeks.

"What is it?" Fabrizio whispered.

Maria shook her head as if not capable of answering.

Fabrizio gazed around the room. In the middle lay a jumble of wooden frames. Sticking out from the heap were heavy metal tubes and one huge screw. There were shallow boxes with multiple small compartments. To Fabrizio it seemed to be little more than a pile of junk.

Scraps of paper lay scattered about, while hundreds of small metal pieces — like wildly sown wheat — were strewn everywhere. And every surface of the room — walls, floor, even the low ceiling — was spotted, stained, and blotched by a dark liquid that dripped and pooled onto the floor like black blood.

"Are your parents here?"

Maria shook her head.

"What's that?" Fabrizio asked, gesturing toward the heap.

Maria sniffed and dabbed at her tears with a strand of her red hair. "Our printing press."

"That's the machine you were talking about? The one that made the papers?"

Maria nodded.

Fabrizio bent over and picked up one of the small metal pieces. It was rectangular, half an inch long, with a notch in its shank and smeared with black goo. There seemed to be something engraved at one end. Fabrizio gazed at it, gradually realizing he was looking at a raised letter, his own name letter, the letter *F*. Backward.

He held it up. "What's this?"

"Type."

"A type . . . of what?"

"A *piece* of type." Maria's voice was thick with frustration. "A letter."

Fabrizio tried to shake the metal bit off his fingers, but the black ooze made it stick. He had to pick it off.

"What's . . . what's all this black stuff?" he asked.

"Ink."

Fabrizio looked at Maria quizzically, then bent over and poked a finger into one of the dark pools. His finger came up black. He smelled it. It had a sweet, oily odor. When he wiped it off on his tunic, it left a dark smear.

"Why would someone destroy our printing press?" asked Maria.

"Maybe so no one would know how you made the papers. Perhaps DeLaBina." He waited for her to say something. She only sniffed.

"Maria — I have to go to my master's house. I need to see if he really got out of the prison and returned home. He probably doesn't want to see me, but I'd feel better knowing he's there. Since your parents aren't here . . . maybe we should go together."

When she made no response, Fabrizio peeked out through the front shutters and then the back. "Soldiers still front and back," he reported.

Maria shrugged with indifference.

Fabrizio wandered around and found steep ladderlike steps leading up to the second floor. Upstairs there were two rooms, each with a rumpled bed, some chests, and small windows.

In one ceiling Fabrizio noticed a small, recessed square. He studied it for a moment before going back down. He found Maria kneeling beside the printing press wreckage, trying to fit two pieces together.

"I think it can be mended." She sounded more hopeful.

"Good." Fabrizio was not very interested. "I'm pretty sure I found a way to get out without being seen. I'll show you."

Maria put the pieces together and followed Fabrizio up to one of the bedrooms.

"My parents' room," she said softly.

Fabrizio pointed to the square cut into the ceiling. "I'm sure that opens. We can get out that way."

"What if my parents come home?"

"You don't know when that might be. It could even be tomorrow."

Maria's eyes welled with tears.

"I promise," said Fabrizio. "We'll only go see if my master got home. Then we'll come back. I just don't think you should stay alone."

Maria sighed. "All right," she said.

The two of them lifted the chest onto the bed. Maria climbed up and was able to push the square to one side. Above was nothing but blue sky.

Maria grabbed the rim of the opening and hoisted herself up and out. Once atop the roof, she lay flat and reached down to help Fabrizio. In moments, they were both on the roof.

Fabrizio looked around. "This way," he said.

They scampered over the roofs to the corner house. The old grapevine had grown high, curled over the roof, and attached itself to the corner chimney.

Fabrizio lay on his stomach and shook the vine. "It should hold us."

He grabbed the thickest part of the vine, swung a foot down, and felt about until he was sure he had support. Once he did, he climbed down, the leaves hiding him from view. In moments he reached the street. Maria soon joined him.

With Fabrizio leading the way, they ran until they had reached Mangus's house. Fabrizio rushed to the door, but when he tried to open it, it would not budge.

He pounded on it. When there was still no reply, he pounded again.

After a few moments they heard the sound of a shifting bolt inside. The door eased open a crack. An eye peered out.

"It's me, Fabrizio! Let me in!"

The door swung all the way open. Standing there was Prince Cosimo.

# CHAPTER 18

$\mathbb{F}$ABRIZIO BACKED AWAY FROM THE DOOR. MARIA, JUST behind him, asked, "Who is it?"

"The king's son," Fabrizio whispered. "The one who sent me to be executed."

Prince Cosimo stood in the doorway, staring at Fabrizio. Though he was dressed as elegantly as when Fabrizio last saw him in the Hall of Justice, he seemed uncertain what to do. He kept fingering his thin mustache, while his gaze shifted nervously from Fabrizio to Maria, then back again. His eyes were ringed by darkness.

"My . . . lord . . ." Fabrizio managed to say, "is my master, Signor Mangus . . . here?"

"I thought . . . you were . . . gone."

"Gone, my lord? With permission, I'm . . . right here."

The prince hesitated, then, as if making up his mind, he abruptly beckoned the boy inside.

Fabrizio stepped forward, turning to include Maria. She looked at the prince, asking permission. When he gave a curt nod, she pressed in close to her friend.

The prince shut the door and bolted it. "Go into your master's study," he commanded.

"Is . . . he all right?" asked Fabrizio.

"Didn't you hear me?" barked Cosimo. "Go!"

"Yes, my lord." Fabrizio, making sure Maria stayed with him, went forward. When he reached Mangus's study, he looked back.

The prince was watching him intently.

Fabrizio darted a glance at Maria, held his breath, and pulled the door open.

Light from the skull's glowing eyes revealed books scattered, and papers and parchment strewn helter-skelter. On the table lay an open book. Fabrizio recognized it as the magic book he'd been secretly studying.

He turned around. Prince Cosimo had followed them into the room and was watching them closely. His face was tense, his eyes wide.

*He's frightened,* thought Fabrizio. "My lord, do you know where my master is?"

"Did . . . did he not send you here?" said the prince.

"The last time I saw him was in a prison cell. In the Hall of Justice."

"Ah! Well, yes, I visited him there, too. He . . . he told me that he believed Magistrato DeLaBina made these treasonous papers. That he was being used by the magistrato for his own reasons." The prince gestured toward the papers that still lay on the table.

"I asked him if he would make that accusation to His Majesty. When he said he would, I . . . I left him in search of a more comfortable room. When I returned . . . he was gone. Vanished. Magic, I thought. After all, he is a magician, isn't he? He should have stayed. I . . . I was trying to help him."

"My lord," said Fabrizio, "we think we saw him beyond the hall, walking through the fog."

"Did you!"

"He was with someone," Maria added.

"Who?" cried the prince, clearly alarmed.

"We couldn't see," said Fabrizio. "It was too foggy, and the people were wearing black robes. Like that one."

Fabrizio pointed to a robe that hung by the side of the door.

The prince shifted from foot to foot. He was growing more agitated. "Very well. I'll tell you what happened to your master."

"Do you know?"

"I fear —"

"Has he been killed?" cried Fabrizio.

The prince started to speak, stopped, and then said, "I believe Count Scarazoni took him away to the Castello."

"Scarazoni!" Fabrizio and Maria said at the same time.

"You said you saw him with someone. I've no doubt it was Scarazoni."

"But why?" asked Fabrizio.

"The count intends to put Mangus on trial." The prince's voice was growing more confident.

"Trial! For what reason?"

"Everyone knows magic is illegal in Pergamontio. My father fears it greatly. He believes what DeLaBina said, that

Mangus made those papers, magically, on behalf of some-one. I'm quite sure that *someone* is Scarazoni. He's trying to overthrow my father. To conceal the truth and to protect himself, the count is . . . prepared to sacrifice your master. If your master is found guilty of doing magic, he'll be put to death.

"Alas," concluded the prince, "I can only do so much. My father has great trust in Scarazoni. I'm afraid he won't believe me if *I* tell him Scarazoni is the traitor. There . . . there's only one way your master can save himself."

Fabrizio struggled to make sense of the prince's words. "How?"

"Mangus must force the count to confess his crime."

"Is that why Scarazoni took my master, to keep him from doing that?"

"That appears to be so," said the prince.

Fabrizio, trying to absorb all the prince had said, looked around. He glanced at the open book of magic. "My lord," he asked, "why are you here?"

"It's my duty to protect the king. Believing your master is innocent, I came here in search of evidence to establish his innocence. In the same fashion I sent you to be executed — to protect you."

"Protect me from whom, my lord?"

"Count Scarazoni. And Magistrato DeLaBina. It was I who told the king to release you."

"Was it?" said Fabrizio. "I thank you. I thought it was the king. But, my lord, perhaps you don't know: DeLaBina is dead."

*"Dead?"* cried the prince.

"Murdered," said Maria.

The prince seemed at a loss for words. "How do you know?"

"We saw his body, my lord," said Fabrizio.

"There was . . . a dagger in his back," Maria added.

"When . . . when did this happen?" asked the prince.

"Last midnight," said Maria.

"Have you . . . have you any idea who did it?"

"We heard DeLaBina arguing with someone in the halls," said Fabrizio.

"And," said Maria, "we saw the hilt of the dagger that killed him. It was covered with red rubies."

The prince looked grave. "A dagger like that belongs to King Claudio."

"My lord," said Fabrizio, "do you think someone stole it?"

"The count and the magistrato were trying to wrest power from His Majesty. But they quarreled. I have no doubt — the count stole my father's dagger and killed DeLaBina."

"A short time later we think we spoke to the one who killed him."

"Did you?" The prince placed his hand on his dagger as if prepared to act. "Who was it?"

"My lord," said Maria, "we didn't see his face. He was wrapped in a black robe."

"Scarazoni wears such a robe," said the prince.

"If you say so," said Fabrizio.

"And now," the prince continued, "the count has your master. Not only do I fear for his life, but King Claudio is in great danger." He moved toward the door. "I need to warn him."

"My lord!" called Fabrizio. "Will you tell him you believe that my master is innocent? That Scarazoni is the true enemy?"

The prince hesitated. "The count is very powerful. But I will try."

"Thank you, my lord," said Fabrizio. "Just one more question. The other night when my master performed at the Sign of the Crown, were you there? In a black robe? Like that." He pointed to the one that hung on the wall.

"Of course not," said the prince. "I don't usually mingle with common people." The prince stepped into the hallway.

"At that performance," said Fabrizio, following after him, "there was another black robe. We don't know who he was."

"Does it matter?" said the prince.

"That black robe sent a warning to my master."

The prince swung around. "A warning about what?"

"He said, 'Tell your master he's in grave danger.'"

The prince stared at Fabrizio, then abruptly

turned back down the hall, only to pause and say, "Boy, let us hope Mangus can convince the king that Scarazoni is guilty. Only that will save his life. As for your own safety, I advise you, beyond all else, avoid Scarazoni. He won't hesitate a moment before killing you, too."

# CHAPTER 19

FABRIZIO STOOD IN THE DOORWAY TO HIS MASTER'S STUDY, staring after the prince. When he was sure Cosimo was gone, he returned to Mangus's table. He picked up one of the treasonous papers, stared at it, and then put it down. "If we believe what the prince said, it must have been Scarazoni — along with DeLaBina — who wanted these made."

Maria, who was behind the table, said, "He didn't convince me. I thought he was making things up as he spoke."

"The place is a mess. He said he came here to look for something to prove Master's innocence. But why would he be going through Master's magic books?"

"Maybe he believes in it," said Maria. "He was nervous and frightened. Fabrizio, do you think he really didn't know that DeLaBina was killed?"

"He acted surprised," said Fabrizio. "I keep thinking about what he said, that he visited my master in his cell. Maria! The man who was with DeLaBina right before he was murdered, didn't he say he visited Mangus in his cell? And did you notice the prince's boots?"

"No."

"They were red. Master Mangus told me, 'Pay attention to what's visible and you can discover what's hidden.' That black robe we met — right after DeLaBina was killed — was completely covered except for the tip of one boot. A *red* boot.

"Another thing," said Fabrizio, growing more excited, "the king's dagger. I just remembered. When I stood before the king, I saw the prince take it. I didn't see him return it." He stared at the skull on the table. "Maria, do you think the prince killed DeLaBina?"

"And is now trying to blame Scarazoni."

"Except, according to the prince, it was Scarazoni who took my master to the Castello. . . ." Fabrizio didn't finish his thought.

"Couldn't you go to the count, tell him what we've discovered, and plead for your master?" said Maria.

"But — what if the prince is right?" said Fabrizio. "He warned us to avoid Scarazoni. Maria, the count is really frightening." Full of gloom, he sank down into Mangus's chair.

After a while, Maria said, "Fabrizio, is there something to eat? Even some bread. It's been a long time since I've eaten."

Fabrizio got up and led Maria out. "There should be food in the kitchen."

He stopped at the doorway and stared at the black robe that hung on the wall.

"Maria," he said, "look!" A piece of type clung to the sleeve of the cloak. Fabrizio plucked it off. It felt sticky.

"Fabrizio, it has to be one of ours. There's no other printing press in the city."

"This is Giuseppe's robe. He's my master's servant."

"How would he get the type?"

"We'd better ask him." Fabrizio led the way to the kitchen shed. "Hello!" he called.

Giuseppe poked his head out of the inner room. "You!" he cried upon seeing Fabrizio. "How did you get here? You were arrested."

"I was able to get free."

"How?"

"With permission, Signore. The door was open."

"Idiot! And what are you doing with my robe?"

"I was just bringing it to you," said Fabrizio.

Giuseppe snatched it. "Who's the filthy girl?"

"My friend Maria. Signor Giuseppe, we haven't eaten since yesterday. Can we get something?"

"Take what you want." Giuseppe started to retreat into his room.

"With permission, have you heard what happened to Master?"

Giuseppe hesitated. "He's being held in the Hall of Justice."

Benito came into the room and said, "For treason."

"He's not a traitor," Fabrizio said hotly. "Not even Prince Cosimo believes Master is guilty."

"How would you know?" said Benito.

"He was just here. He told us."

Giuseppe and Benito exchanged looks of alarm.

Fabrizio noticed that Benito was holding a full sack. "Signore, are you going somewhere?"

"We're leaving Pergamontio," said Giuseppe. He hurried into the inner room.

"Did he say you're *leaving*?" Fabrizio asked Benito.

Benito nodded. "We no longer wish to be associated with Mangus."

Giuseppe reappeared holding a bulging sack of his own. "Besides, we've made enough money to be independent."

"How?"

The two servants grinned. "I was working for the Primo Magistrato DeLaBina," said Giuseppe.

"And I for Count Scarazoni."

"Since when?" cried an astonished Fabrizio.

"I met with DeLaBina the other night, right after Master's performance," said Giuseppe.

"And I with the count," said Benito.

"But why?" said Fabrizio.

"The magistrato wished to know what Mangus did at his performance. I told him — for a price."

Benito grinned. "As for me, the count wished to know about the magistrato."

"So it was you who told DeLaBina about Master's 'making something from nothing'! And me collecting the papers!"

Giuseppe laughed. "He pays well."

Fabrizio turned to Benito. "What did you tell the count?"

Benito was unable to hide his amusement. "Giuseppe told me what DeLaBina was doing and I told Scarazoni. Didn't we tell you servants run the world? Good-bye."

The two headed for the door.

"Signor Giuseppe! Signor Benito," Fabrizio called after them. "Perhaps you didn't know Magistrato DeLaBina was murdered last night."

The servants swung around.

"We found him," said Maria.

They stood openmouthed.

"It's true," said Fabrizio.

"Who . . . who killed him?" said Benito.

"The prince told us it was Count Scarazoni. And to protect himself Scarazoni is accusing Master. He took Master to the Castello."

Benito, looking ill, pulled at Giuseppe's arm. "We need to get out of the city fast."

Fabrizio held up the piece of type. "We found this sticking to that robe of yours."

"It's from my house," said Maria. "Signor Giuseppe, do you know anything about DeLaBina going to a house on the Street of the Wood Sellers and destroying something there?"

"Giuseppe, we must leave now!" cried Benito.

Giuseppe held back. "You two need to understand what kind of friends we have. Yes, I was asked to go to a house to pull apart some machine."

"Early this morning?" said Fabrizio. "In the fog?"

"Exactly so. I met someone outside the Hall of Justice. He sent me."

"Who was it?"

"When you're given orders by higher-ups, you don't

look at their faces, just their money. I can assure you, I saw a lot."

"Giuseppe and I," bragged Benito, "only deal with powerful people."

"The one who sent me to that house," said Giuseppe, "told me he spoke for the king."

"The king!" cried Fabrizio.

"Did he wear a black robe?" asked Maria.

"What of it?" said Giuseppe. "I wear one, too."

"Why did this person ask you?" Maria said.

"He knew I worked for DeLaBina."

"Is that why the prince was here?" cried Fabrizio, finally understanding. "To pay you off?"

Benito yanked at Giuseppe again. "You're talking too much!"

Giuseppe glared at Fabrizio. "Say anything about this and you'll find yourself in great trouble."

Maria glared at the servants. "What you destroyed belonged to my parents. Do you know where they are?"

"That house was deserted when I got there," said Giuseppe.

"No soldiers?" asked Fabrizio.

"Of course not. I wouldn't have been able to get in. Now keep your mouths shut. Both of you! Just remember how powerful our friends are." He shook a fist. The two servants ran off.

# CHAPTER 20

**I** THINK THINGS ARE GETTING EVEN WORSE FOR MASTER," said Fabrizio as he watched the servants run off.

Maria, meanwhile, had found a loaf of bread, tore off a piece, and offered some to Fabrizio. Then she uncovered a hunk of cheese. They shared that, too.

"The awful thing is," said Fabrizio, who had been trying to sort things out in his mind, "I really don't know if we should believe everything the prince said. Or any of it. And Giuseppe suggested he was sent to your house by the king." He shook his head. "My master told me it's best to find the simplest solution, but this seems so complicated."

"Do we know anything for sure?" asked Maria.

"We need to think it out," said Fabrizio. The two went back to Mangus's study. While Maria sat behind the table, Fabrizio walked around, putting things back in place.

"Just a few nights ago, at my master's performance," he began, "somebody warned him that he was in danger. Two days later, DeLaBina came barging into this room. And now . . . he's dead."

"That we certainly know," agreed Maria.

"My master thought DeLaBina didn't really care about the *making* of the papers. That he was after someone else, some 'devilish' person who asked that those papers be made."

"That was Scarazoni, right?" said Maria.

Fabrizio nodded. "At least DeLaBina wanted my master to say it was Scarazoni who told him to make the papers. The prince wants the same thing. But Mangus didn't make the papers. And Scarazoni didn't tell him to make them."

"It was DeLaBina," said Maria, "who asked my parents to make them."

"Then somebody killed DeLaBina."

"Your master needs to have some friends," said Maria.

Fabrizio shoved a few books onto shelves. "Maria!" he suddenly said. "That person in a black robe who warned me that my master was in danger. He seemed to know what the magistrato was planning. If we could find out who that person is, maybe we could discover a friend."

"How can we do that?"

"At the Sign of the Crown, where the performance took place, the tavern owner, Signor Galda, is Master's good friend. Maybe he knows who that black robe was. I think I know how I can ask him."

It did not take long for them to run to the Sign of the Crown. Inside, the dim air was thick with the stench of sour wine and stale garlic. Cured Parma hams hung on the walls. In one corner stood a large basket of fresh-made bread, its yeasty smell inviting.

There were only a few patrons. Off to one side, Signor Galda was sitting at a small table. In the gloom of the room his bald head gleamed as he bent in close conversation with an elderly man.

Fabrizio and Maria approached. "Signor Galda . . ."

Galda turned and smiled. But the moment he realized who had spoken he scowled. "What do you want?"

"With permission, Signor Galda, I am Master Mangus's servant, and —"

"I know perfectly well who you are," said Galda.

"My master wishes to know the best night for his next magic performance."

Galda frowned. "You may tell your master he's *not* welcome here anymore. I'll have nothing to do with those who dabble in magic. And you can also tell him I wish he had never performed his evil arts in my establishment. Now, get out of here!" He rose up from his chair, threatening.

Taken completely by surprise, Fabrizio stepped back. "But, Signore —!"

"Out!" Galda pointed to the door.

"Signor Galda, with permission ... one more question."

"What is it?"

"The other night, at my master's performance, there was someone in the audience wearing a black robe. Do you know who it was?"

Galda remained silent for a moment. Then he said, "I thought he was a monk. He wasn't, and it explains my anger."

"Forgive me, Signore. I don't understand."

"The morning after Mangus's performance, Count Scarazoni came here. He informed me that he — in a black robe — had been at the performance."

"Scarazoni!" cried Fabrizio and Maria simultaneously.

"None other. He ordered me never to allow magic again. Furthermore, if I did not forbid such events he would lock my doors. Now do you understand? So please leave and tell your master not to come back!"

Fabrizio and Maria hurried out to the street. After walking a few paces, Fabrizio said, "So it *was* Count Scarazoni who gave me that warning."

"But the prince said DeLaBina and Scarazoni were working together," said Maria.

"Benito and Giuseppe seemed to suggest that," agreed Fabrizio. "But, then, everyone is blaming the count. Except if Scarazoni warned my master, doesn't that mean he's our friend?"

"Yet the prince said the count took away your master so he could accuse him of being the traitor," said Maria. "Another thing. Why would Scarazoni's soldiers be sent to my house *after* they broke up the machine?"

"And," said an exasperated Fabrizio, "don't forget the king wanted me to be executed right away. The truth is, everybody seems to be lying!" He slapped his head with frustration. "It's what people say: Just because you think you know everything doesn't mean you know anything."

They walked toward Mangus's house in silence.

"Fabrizio," said Maria, "tell me about the message the king sent to the executioner. The one that asked for your immediate death."

"The king sent and signed it. Fortunately, the executioner couldn't read. So when I read it I said the king was freeing me."

Maria stopped. "Fabrizio, you told me you didn't read."

Fabrizio's cheeks grew warm. "I do. A little."

"Are you sure you read that message correctly?"

"I tried . . ."

"Could you write out what was on the note? Along with the signature you saw?"

"Maybe."

They rushed back to Mangus's house and into his study. Once there, Fabrizio picked up a writing quill and dipped it into a bottle of ink. After thinking very hard, he carefully wrote what he remembered on a scrap of parchment. He handed it to Maria. She drew the skull lantern closer to see.

*Letthe boy escapedeath S*

She looked up. "You wrote, 'Let the boy escape death S.'"

"You mean the word I couldn't read was 'escape'? And the signature was an *S*?"

"If what you've written is accurate."

"Then Scarazoni was setting me free! But why?" Fabrizio leaned over the table and gazed at what he had written. He put his finger to the letters and traced them, silently mouthing each sound.

As he did, a pounding erupted on the front door.

"Someone for my master," said Fabrizio. "I'll send whoever it is away."

He hurried to the front door and pulled it open only to gasp. Standing there was a man wrapped in a black robe.

# CHAPTER 21

$\mathfrak{T}$HE MAN THREW BACK THE HOOD AND REVEALED HIM-
self as Count Scarazoni.

"My lord!" said Fabrizio, so startled that he forgot
to bow.

Count Scarazoni glared at him. "I've come to speak
to you."

"*Me?*"

"You."

"Yes . . . my lord, of course. Please . . ." Fabrizio
led the count into the study. Maria was standing
behind the table, looking at the count with great alarm.
She turned to Fabrizio. He silently mouthed the name:
*Scarazoni.*

The count scrutinized the room. Seeing the skull, he
stepped forward, reached into it, and pinched out the candle flame. He turned to Fabrizio. "Your master's magic is
false. I don't believe in it."

"He would agree with you, my lord," said Fabrizio,
bowing.

"Nor do I fear him," said the count.

"With permission," returned Fabrizio, "I fear you."

"With reason. Your master is under arrest. He is await-
ing trial by the king. For practicing magic."

"I knew that, my lord."

The count scowled. "It's supposed to be a court secret.
Who told you?"

"Prince Cosimo. He was just here, my lord. A short
time ago."

"I should not be surprised."

"He said you took my master away."

"Me? A lie. Mangus was taken by the king. What other
lies did Cosimo tell you?"

Fabrizio darted a look at Maria. She nodded.

"Answer my question!" barked Scarazoni.

"My lord, he said that you . . . were working in league
with DeLaBina to overthrow the king."

"Prince Cosimo is a fool. Hardly more than a boy.
To think he's the heir to the throne. I should be next in
line." The count glared at Fabrizio as if it were his fault.

"May I remind you, the prince sent you to be executed. It was I who saved you."

Fabrizio bowed. "Yes, my lord, I know that . . . now. My gracious thanks."

"My lord," Maria challenged, "the prince said you had DeLaBina commission my parents to make those treasonous papers."

Scarazoni swung around. "Who is this girl?"

"My friend Maria."

"Has she anything to do with this business?"

Before Fabrizio could speak, Maria said, "I'm the daughter of the people who brought the printing press to Pergamontio. Did you know about that?"

"Of course," said Scarazoni.

"Do you know where my parents are?" Maria demanded.

Scarazoni looked at her coldly. "I do."

"Tell me —!"

"Be quiet!" Scarazoni turned back to Fabrizio. "I've come here to tell you what you must do."

"Me, my lord?"

"I've no particular interest in your master. He's a charlatan. It merely serves my purpose to save him. But I need your help."

"But —"

"It's best I don't speak to him directly. Informers are everywhere in the Castello. I have arranged — secretly — for you to see your master. Tonight. You will tell him that at his trial he must get the prince to confess his crimes. Moreover, he must use his magic to do so."

"Forgive me," said Fabrizio. "Didn't you just say you don't believe my master can do real magic?"

"I don't believe. It's the king who fears devils, ghosts, and magic. The prince, too. Indeed, if your master is found guilty of practicing magic, he'll be put to death. *But*, if he can use his trickery to get the prince to confess, it will convince King Claudio of the truth."

"My lord, I will tell him. But . . . but what do you wish the prince to . . . confess to?"

"That he conspired with DeLaBina to overthrow King Claudio."

"Against his own father?" cried Maria.

"Prince Cosimo and DeLaBina arranged to have those papers made. Knowing the king believes in magic, they claimed your master made them with magic at my request. Their intent? To get rid of me. But DeLaBina made the mistake of bringing you before the king. You insisted your master was innocent. When the king asked you to say who conspired with Mangus, you looked right at the prince."

"I was only wishing he would help me," said Fabrizio.

"He thought you were going to accuse him. That's why he moved to get rid of you. You see what a coward he is. No doubt he feared the magistrato would blunder everything and give him away, too. So Cosimo murdered him. I have no doubt he would have killed your master if the king had not taken him away."

"Please, tell me about my parents," Maria pleaded.

"I have them in a safe place."

"But why . . . ?"

"Originally, to protect them from DeLaBina. Now I might need them to testify against the prince. But only if I have to. I much prefer to keep all information about that

machine of yours a secret. I'll not have a printing press —
or any modern invention — in Pergamontio."

"Did you send Giuseppe to my house to destroy
the press?"

"While I am glad it was destroyed, it was not me. I
believe it was the prince, trying to do away with evidence.
I did send my soldiers there to protect the pieces. I might
have need of them to show how those papers were actually made."

"Forgive me, my lord," said Fabrizio. "I have a question. Was it you who came to this house on the morning of
Mangus's performance?"

"That's how I learned of it."

"Was it you who warned my master — through me —
about DeLaBina?"

"Yes."

"Thank you, my lord," said Fabrizio. "Can I beg you to
release this girl's parents?"

"Please, my lord," added Maria.

"You see the mischief a printing machine can do.

Indeed, if I release your parents, they will have to leave the city."

Maria all but shouted, "We don't want to stay here!"

"Very well," said Scarazoni. "I will seek a way to release them. If" — he looked hard at Fabrizio — "if you agree to tell Mangus he must make the prince confess."

"My lord, wouldn't it be better if you told him your-self? He . . . he doesn't always listen to me."

"If I speak to him, the prince will learn of it. He'll become suspicious and do something rash. No, far better if it is just you."

"I'll try, my lord."

"Good. My carriage will be at your door tonight. It will bring you to Mangus. Tell him what I've commanded."

"My lord," said Fabrizio, "where is he?"

"You will find out."

"With permission, may my friend go, too?"

Scarazoni looked at the girl. "No, she should return to her home."

"Will my parents be there?"

"It depends on this boy," said the count. He turned to Fabrizio. "Be ready at midnight."

"Fabrizio," said Maria after Scarazoni had departed, "can you show me the way home?"

"Do you want to be there alone?" said Fabrizio.

"If my parents return I need to be there. And I'll try to put the press back together."

Fabrizio agreed. As he led the way, neither spoke, each thoughtful about his or her own concerns. When they reached Maria's house it was no longer being guarded. No one was inside.

Maria bid Fabrizio good night, but not before she made him promise he would come back tomorrow to tell her all that happened.

"If I can," he said, and started off.

"Fabrizio!" she called after him. "Be very careful!"

# CHAPTER 22

𝕿HE CATHEDRAL BELLS HAD BARELY CHIMED THE MID-
night hour when Fabrizio, fully dressed and sleeping but
fitfully on the floor near the front door, heard a sharp rap.
He jumped up and peered out. A green-coated court soldier holding a partially hooded lantern stood on the narrow,
dark street before the house. Behind him loomed a carriage
with four black horses in its traces. At the reins was another
soldier.

Fabrizio stepped from the house. One of the soldiers
held the carriage door open. Fabrizio climbed in. The
moment he did, the door clicked shut.

Having never been in a carriage before, Fabrizio looked
around. The cab was gloomy and damp, smelling of moldy
leather and sweat. Two seats with wool-leaking cushions
faced each other. An unlit candle had been stuck in a wall
socket. Fabrizio squeezed into a corner.

No sooner did he settle himself than the carriage
lurched forward, swaying and bouncing as it went. He had
to put a hand to the carriage wall to keep his place.

Trying not to be fearful, Fabrizio looked out the small window. All he could see was an occasional burning candle in a solitary window.

The carriage went upward, groaning and squeaking. The steady clip-clop of the horses' hooves on street stones soon settled into a boring rhythm. The repetition dulled Fabrizio's senses. The hour was late. He nodded off.

With a jolt, the carriage stopped. On the instant, Fabrizio became alert. The cab door flew open. A soldier poked his head in. "Out!" he ordered.

"Where are we?" whispered a frightened Fabrizio.

"Out!"

Fabrizio stepped out into swirling mist. Two soldiers stood waiting, one of them holding a lit lamp. A gust of wind caused the flame to dance wickedly. "Follow me," the soldier ordered. Fabrizio hesitated only to receive a sharp jab in his back.

As they walked through the mist, he saw that they were moving along the base of a stone wall. He looked up. The wall seemed to melt overhead into the dark clouds. Looking down he saw a scattering of small lights — as if heaven had fallen.

The soldier stopped. His lamplight revealed a small, low door built into the wall. He unlocked it with a large key, then handed his lamp to Fabrizio. "Walk forward. You'll be met."

"Where am I going?" Fabrizio asked.

"Just go."

Having no choice, Fabrizio passed through the small entryway. The door slammed shut behind him. A lock turned.

He held up the light. A low, narrow tunnel stretched before him. Its walls were built of crudely cut stone, the floor surfaced with jagged, ill-fitting stones and pebbles. Fabrizio was reminded of the passage to the executioner. *Am I headed to the same kind of place?*

Taking deep breaths to keep calm, Fabrizio walked in the only direction he could, forward. After some fifty yards, he stepped out of the tunnel, held up his lamp, and gasped. He had come into a cavelike room with a domed ceiling and a few entrances. Heaped against the ancient walls were tall mounds of mottled human bones and skulls.

Two armed blue-coated law-court soldiers appeared from one of the side entrances.

*The prince must be in charge here,* Fabrizio thought. He grew tenser. Then he saw Mangus standing between the soldiers. Fabrizio was shocked by his appearance. Deep shadows rimmed the old man's eyes. His beard was ill kempt. His clothing was rumpled, the slippers on his feet torn.

Fabrizio took a step forward, only to halt. *Perhaps he will refuse to see me.*

Mangus had yet to realize Fabrizio was there. It took a touch on his arm by one of the guards to make him turn. When he saw the boy, his mouth fell open.

Fabrizio was sure he saw disappointment on the old man's face.

"They only told me that someone was coming to see me," said Mangus. "I was hoping it would be my good wife." Tears came into his eyes. "But you — like your beloved magic — *you* always reappear."

"Forgive me, Master," said Fabrizio, not sure he should even call him that. "Mistress is still away." He started forward again, only to halt. "Are they treating you well?"

"I'm alive. That's not something everyone here can say." Mangus gestured around him. "An ancient burial crypt. A fitting place for my trial, don't you think?"

"Is it to be here?"

"I fear so."

"When?" asked Fabrizio.

"Tomorrow night."

"Tomorrow!"

Mangus turned to one of the soldiers. "Am I permitted to speak privately?"

"Briefly." The two guards stepped back a few paces.

Mangus, his back to the soldiers but facing Fabrizio, touched a finger to his lips: *caution*.

Fabrizio, understanding, gave a tiny nod of response. "Master," he said, stepping closer so he could speak in a low voice, "Count Scarazoni arranged for me to come. He bid me tell you . . . that if you can get Prince Cosimo to confess that he conspired to have those papers made, the count will help you. Otherwise things will go badly."

Mangus sighed. "Is that why he sent you here, to tell me that?"

"Yes, Master."

"Is that true — about Cosimo?"

"I think so. I met with him, too."

"You've led a busy life since I dismissed you," said Mangus.

"Prince Cosimo said you must get Scarazoni to confess to the same thing."

Mangus lifted his hands as if to say, "Absurd."

"Master, I discovered how those papers were made. After I left you in the Hall of Justice, I met a girl — Maria. She explained how she — and her parents — printed the papers on something called a . . . a printing press. It's a machine that can imitate writing. It makes many copies. All the same."

"I have heard rumors of such a machine," said Mangus. "A German invention. The rumors sounded too" — he shrugged — "magical. Did you actually see one? In Pergamontio?"

"In a way. It was broken up. And, Master," said Fabrizio, feeling he had to hurry with his news, "DeLaBina was murdered."

"Murdered! How so?"

Fabrizio told him about finding the body.

"Who committed this crime?"

Fabrizio, looking beyond Mangus to the soldiers, was afraid to say. They appeared to be listening.

Mangus seemed to understand. "Well, there is much lying in the world."

"It's what people say," agreed Fabrizio. "When liars are found, truth is hidden."

Mangus gazed at the boy.

"Master, forgive me. There is even more." Fabrizio told him what Signor Galda had said.

Mangus sighed. "Now even if — by some miracle —

I regain my freedom, I shall have no way of making a living."

"But, Master," said Fabrizio, "there's another thing people say: 'If you have to choose between knowing your friends or enemies, better to know your friends.'"

Mangus considered Fabrizio. "True."

"With permission, Master, I have some more news." He told Mangus about Benito and Giuseppe.

As Mangus listened, his shoulders slumped. He took a deep breath. "Where are they now?"

"I don't know. They ran off."

"Fabrizio, there's no pain like the pain of betrayal." Mangus closed his eyes briefly, then opened them. "But no joy like the blessing of loyalty. I'm grateful that you've discovered many useful facts. But . . . how were you able to?"

"With permission, Master. My . . . reasoning."

A small smile played upon Mangus's lips. He reached out and grasped Fabrizio's arm. He was about to speak when they realized that Prince Cosimo was in the room. How long he had been there, or how he had learned of his visit, Fabrizio had no idea. He did recall the count's warning, that the Castello was full of informers.

"Boy!" cried the prince. "Did you give the magician my message?" He kept his distance from Mangus.

"Yes, my lord," said Fabrizio.

"Good." The prince made a motion with his hand. The guard drew in. "Then he must return to his cell."

Fabrizio turned back to Mangus. "Master, what can I do to help you?"

Before Mangus could speak, Prince Cosimo called out, "Remind Signor Mangus that the penalty for practicing magic in Pergamontio is death."

Mangus turned. "My lord . . ."

"Indeed," said the prince, ignoring Mangus and addressing Fabrizio, "I suggest you bring a coffin to the trial."

"A coffin!" cried Fabrizio.

"He may need it," said the prince.

The guards were now holding Mangus's arms. The old man stared so at Fabrizio, the boy was certain he was trying to tell him something.

"Yes, Fabrizio," he suddenly said. "Bring *my* coffin."

"If you say so, Master," replied Fabrizio, trying to understand.

"Has there been any word from my wife?" called Mangus as the guards began to move him away. "Has she been told what has happened?"

"Master, I don't know." Fabrizio turned to the prince. "Might I visit again?"

"Tomorrow," said a grinning Cosimo, "is his trial. So be sure to bring the coffin."

# CHAPTER 23

**S**ICK WITH SORROW, STARING GLUMLY AT THE GROUND, Fabrizio made his way slowly back through the tunnel. His head filled with random thoughts: *There must be some way to help Master. Why was Master agreeing about the coffin? The prince, like his father, is frightened of Master. If I knew magic, I could take care of him!*

As he neared the outer door, Fabrizio looked up. Standing there — illuminated by a soldier holding a torch — were a man and a woman.

The woman was short and plump with graying red hair hanging down on either side of her face like parting curtains. Her dress was black, though she wore a dark green shawl over her shoulders. The man next to her was somewhat taller, barrel-chested, slightly stooped, and with a narrow, red-bearded face. Fierce green eyes looked out from beneath bushy red eyebrows.

The man made a stiff bow. "I am Signor Roberto Zeanzi," he announced. "My wife, the Signora Avella Zeanzi."

"Signore," said Fabrizio. "I don't know who you are."

"We," said the man, "are Maria's parents."

Fabrizio's face broke into a wide smile. "Ah, Signore, Signora! I'm so glad to meet you. But it's nothing compared to what Maria will feel. My name is Fabrizio, and she and I have become good friends."

"Is she all right?" her father asked.

"She's fine, Signore," said Fabrizio.

"Count Scarazoni said you would know where she was," said Maria's mother.

"She's at your home. Waiting for you. But where were you?"

The woman, with a hasty, nervous glance at the soldier, only said, "Count Scarazoni."

The soldier opened the tunnel door. "This way," he said.

They stepped into the windy night. The soldier, holding up his fluttering torch, guided them to the carriage. As soon as they climbed into the cab, the carriage began to move.

"We know very little about this business," said Maria's

father, leaning forward toward Fabrizio and speaking low. "We were prisoners."

"Count Scarazoni took us away," added Signora Zeanzi. "He claimed it was for our own protection."

"A violent man," said her husband.

As the carriage went along, Fabrizio told Maria's parents all that had happened.

"DeLaBina murdered," said Signor Zeanzi when Fabrizio was finished. "Maria, you, and your master imprisoned. All this because of what we printed!"

"And I'm afraid," said Fabrizio, "we think the prince had your machine broken apart to destroy the evidence as to how those papers were made."

"Broken!" cried Maria's mother.

"Maria thinks she can put it back together again."

"It's strange to us," said Signor Zeanzi, "how so many here still believe in magic."

The carriage came to a stop. Signora Zeanzi looked out the window. "We're home," she said to her husband. Even as she spoke, the door flung open and a gleeful Maria ran out. There was a warm reunion, cut short by the carriage driver's insistence — to Fabrizio — that he needed to move on.

Just before Fabrizio climbed back into the carriage, Maria rushed up to him. "Is your master safe?"

"It's not certain."

"Come by tomorrow and tell me everything that happened."

Fabrizio promised that if possible he would, then he let the carriage take him home.

As the carriage trundled along, Fabrizio reminded himself that the house would be deserted. *How strange! Alone in that house. But Master has it worse.*

It was still dark when Fabrizio stepped out of the carriage. Eager to get some sleep, he watched the carriage clatter away, then turned to the house and pushed the door. It would not budge.

Had he locked it? From the outside that was impossible. Gazing up, he saw the light of a burning candle in a window on the second floor. Had Benito or Giuseppe returned?

Upset, Fabrizio knocked on the door.

After a moment a voice called, "Who is it?"

Fabrizio stood before the door, trying to guess who was speaking.

"Who is it?" repeated the voice from inside, with more urgency.

"It's me, Fabrizio!"

The door opened.

"Mistress!" cried Fabrizio in a burst of joy. Sophia was dressed in her sleeping gown, a cap on her head, her feet bare, and a shawl around her shoulders. In one of her hands was a small candle. Fabrizio snatched her free hand and covered it with kisses. "You don't know how happy I am to see you!"

"Quickly," she urged, looking up and down the street. "Come in!"

As soon as he stepped into the house, Sophia shut and bolted the door. Putting her candle aside, she gave Fabrizio a great hug. "Oh, Fabrizio!" she said, her voice laden with emotion. "I've been so worried. When I heard that Master was arrested I came straight home. But the house was empty. Even Benito and Giuseppe are gone. I've just been sitting here, waiting for someone to come." Her eyes glistened with tears. "Where were you? Where is everybody?"

"I was with Master."

"Bless you," she cried, her face brightening. "Is he well? Where is he?"

"In some crypt near the Castello."

"A crypt!" she gasped. "Have they —?"

"No, no, Mistress, he's alive! But, he's tired and worried. He asked about you just now. But . . . what about your sister?"

"She's not very ill," said Sophia, dismissing the question with a wave of her hand. Leaning back to catch her breath, she closed her eyes. Fabrizio could see her hands were shaking. She roused herself. "Fabrizio, why was Master arrested?"

"Mistress, there's much to tell you."

In Mangus's study Sophia sat behind the table. Fabrizio stood before her, the glowing skull lamp between them. He waited patiently while Sophia — still agitated — clasped her hands in brief prayer. When she regained some calm, she looked up at Fabrizio, smiled gamely, and said, "Now, please, tell me all."

"They claim Master was trying to overthrow the king."

"Overthrow the . . . ! Impossible!" cried Sophia. "Why? Who says so?"

Fabrizio related all that had happened since she had left, finishing with the news about Giuseppe and Benito.

"Is Mangus truly going to be put on trial?"

"I fear so. And, Mistress, I think he expects the worst."

"What is the . . . worst?"

"That he'll be . . . put to death."

Sophia put a hand to her heart. "Fabrizio, whom do you believe? Cosimo or Scarazoni?"

"The count may look like the devil himself, but I believe him."

"When is Master's trial?"

"Tomorrow night."

"Tomorrow!"

"I was told I could be there."

Sophia sighed, picked up one of the treasonous papers from the desk, studied it, and put it down.

"Mistress," Fabrizio said, when she looked up again, "there's something . . . I haven't said."

"Something . . . worse?"

Fabrizio nodded. "Master . . . dismissed me."

"Dismissed you! But . . . why?"

Fabrizio hung his head. "He said . . . there was no future for me with him. That I always made things worse."

"But what did you do?"

Struggling to keep his voice free of emotion, Fabrizio said, "Mistress, I truly tried to be helpful, as you told me to. I really want to stay." His eyes filled with tears.

"When you saw him — just now — how did he receive you?"

"He said nothing about that."

"Did he *refuse* to see you?"

"No, Mistress. Though he'd rather it was you, not me."

Sophia smiled gently. "Fabrizio, he needs you. And *I* need you."

"Thank you, Mistress." Fabrizio smeared away his tears. "You're very kind. But I must tell you, when I was at the crypt and asked Master what I might do for him, before he could answer, Prince Cosimo said, 'Bring him a coffin.'"

"A coffin!" cried Sophia. "Oh, Fabrizio . . . what are we to do?"

"Mistress, I don't know. Count Scarazoni says Master — at his trial — must make the prince confess. That's why I was allowed to see him. To tell him that. Except the prince also said Master must make the *count* confess."

"But . . ."

"Exactly, Mistress," said Fabrizio. "And to do both is impossible, isn't it?"

## CHAPTER 24

Sophia stood up. "You must be exhausted. Have you eaten?"

"Some bread — a long time ago."

"Come."

Fabrizio followed her out of the house, into the courtyard. As they went he glanced at the coffin that sat among the other magic equipment. Just to see it filled him with despair.

In the kitchen Sophia and Fabrizio found some stale bread and sausage. Two wizened apples and a few figs completed their meal.

They ate in silence, glad of the other's company.

After a while, Fabrizio said, "Shall I tell you about the printing press, Mistress?"

"I suppose I should hear," said Sophia, suppressing a yawn. But before Fabrizio could speak, she said, "Fabrizio, why do you think Master agreed that you should bring a coffin?"

"Forgive me, Mistress. I fear he doesn't expect to live."

Sophia struggled to keep from crying. "Fabrizio, we need our sleep."

On the second floor, just before Fabrizio went up the ladder to his attic space, Sophia called, "Fabrizio! I'm glad you're here."

"Thank you, Mistress. As I you."

Fabrizio lay on his straw pallet, arms behind his head, staring up into the darkness. Shifting his head slightly, he saw a star through a crack in the roof. It seemed to wink at him.

He found it impossible to sleep, wishing he could make Master just vanish from that awful crypt. He was sure it was haunted by ghosts. No question it would take magic to free Master. Except Mangus insisted there was no magic. His words, "What I do is *imitation* magic — *illusions*," slipped into Fabrizio's thoughts.

Fabrizio heaved a sigh. He believed in magic, but the only other ones who seemed to were the prince and the king. *In fact, the king is so fearful of magic, he most likely will condemn Master. And if Master is executed, it won't be an illusion. The prince will save himself. No wonder Master agreed I should bring a coffin. He has no hope!*

But gradually a new thought came. *Is it that coffin, the one in the courtyard, that Master wants? For a particular reason?*

Fabrizio grew restless. Deciding he must know the answer before he could sleep, he climbed down the ladder and on to the lower floor. As he passed his master's study he noticed a glow. They had forgotten to snuff out the skull's candle. He decided he could use it.

Holding the skull with two hands — it warmed him — he lit his way. He stepped into the courtyard. A chill breeze made him shiver. Goose bumps prickled his arms. He looked up. In the sky a three-quarter moon hung huge and white. From the east, long fingers of dark clouds reached across the heavens, as if intent upon snatching away the light. Fabrizio read the sky: The weather would be turning stormy.

He held up the skull and gazed about the courtyard. The coffin, which rested on a pair of trestles, was made of white pine, with three iron handles on each side. The lid was level with his chin.

Fabrizio ran his hand over the coffin's smooth lid, noticing that it had rusty hinges. Setting the skull to one side, Fabrizio wedged his fingers under the lid, only to halt. *Maybe someone's inside.* In haste, he made the sign of the cross over his heart.

Steady again, feet braced, he pushed the lid open. The rusty hinges creaked. Their stiffness kept the lid up.

Using the skull light, Fabrizio peered inside. The coffin was empty. Feeling simultaneously relief and disappointment, he dropped down onto the flats of his feet.

Then he realized he *had* seen something. Not sure what it was, he set the skull inside the coffin and examined the interior again. There it was: two holes on the coffin bottom. They were at the head end and to the left side. Each hole was about an inch wide.

Fabrizio bent over and looked underneath. The holes did not go through. *That was strange.*

Then he realized there was, barely visible, a thin,

straight crack running the entire length of the coffin's bottom. It was not centered, but was three-quarters of the way from the left side.

Sliding the skull light to the narrow side of the crack, Fabrizio stuck his fingers into the holes and yanked. *Pop!* Two-thirds of the coffin bottom came up.

He stared. The bottom he had first observed was false. Beneath that false bottom was a space seven inches deep. Fabrizio tried to make sense of his discovery. Suddenly, he understood: The space was meant to conceal someone. Those holes were for breathing!

Fabrizio went back through the courtyard and climbed to his place beneath the attic roof. As he lay on his pallet, eyes open, he watched the star through the crack. Mangus's words filled his thoughts: "What I do is *imitation* magic — *illusions.*"

Gradually, Fabrizio thought out a plan to save Mangus. It was, he realized, a very dangerous plan. But what else could he do?

# CHAPTER 25

In the morning, drops of water slipping through a crack in the roof and splashing his face woke Fabrizio. The steady beat of rain rattled overhead. From a distance thunder rumbled. His plan for rescuing Master Mangus filled his thoughts.

He scrambled down from his loft and looked into the bedroom. Mistress wasn't there. Alarmed, he all but tumbled to the first floor and looked out the front door. Rain was sluicing along the street stones and flushing dirt down the central gutter. Across the way, huddled against a recessed door, stood two of Scarazoni's green-coated soldiers. Their uniforms were dark with rain.

Fabrizio slammed the door shut and rushed into Mangus's study. Mercifully, Mistress was seated at Master's table, studying one of the treasonous papers.

"Mistress. There are soldiers outside. Watching us."

Sophia looked up. "I saw. I suppose as long as they stay outside we needn't worry."

"Maybe Scarazoni is protecting us."

"A good thing."

"Mistress," said an impatient Fabrizio, "last night, after I went to my place, I thought of a way to help Master."

"Did you?"

"I'll tell you, but first I need to explain how those papers were made."

"Fabrizio, this isn't the —"

"Mistress, you need to know. It's part of my idea."

"Very well."

Fabrizio explained about the printing press. "People in Pergamontio don't know about it. To see all those papers — exactly alike — it seemed like magic to everyone. I thought so. Even Master was puzzled."

"I'm sure it's a marvel. But what has it to do with your plan?"

"The crypt, where Master's trial will be held, don't you think it must be haunted?"

"Fabrizio —"

"The king and the prince both believe in magic," Fabrizio rushed on. "And ghosts. The king believes those papers were made by magic. He's very fearful. So is the prince."

To Mistress's questioning look, Fabrizio said, "It's true. When DeLaBina took me before the king, I heard the king say so. I saw it, too."

"Fabrizio, just tell me your idea!"

"It's this: Master agreed that we bring that coffin from the courtyard. I wondered why. Last night, after you went to sleep, I examined it. Mistress, it has a false bottom."

"True. Though he hasn't used it much."

"But *we* can!" And Fabrizio went on to outline his plan.

When he was done, Sophia stared at him.

"Don't you think it just might convince the king?" Fabrizio added.

Sophia remained thoughtfully silent.

"Perhaps, Mistress," Fabrizio coaxed, "Master was thinking the same thing."

"I admit," Sophia said after a while, "I can't suggest a better way. And, as you say, maybe Master did have the same idea. Still," she warned, "it's very dangerous. We'll need to plan with the greatest care."

Fabrizio shrugged. "As they say, to plan well is to tell the future."

"When would I reveal myself?"

"You'd have to listen, and decide for yourself."

"A great deal will depend on that," said Sophia thoughtfully. "If we don't do it well, Fabrizio, if we're uncovered, it will go very badly for both of us — and Master. At the least, you might become homeless. The same for me."

"But, Mistress, we'll have done *something*."

"If we are successful, it will be you who will have saved us."

Fabrizio grinned. "Then Master might allow me to stay."

Sophia smiled gently. "I will insist upon it." She quickly became serious. "Very well, we must begin. I suppose you know where to find your friend Maria."

"I do, Mistress."

"Go there. Quickly. Find out if that . . ."

"Printing machine."

". . . can work. Ask her father if he will print some copies of this."

She searched among the table's clutter, found a scrap of parchment, picked up a quill, sharpened it with a knife, dipped the point into the ink pot, and began to write on the scrap.

Fabrizio, watching her, was suddenly full of doubt. "Mistress," he whispered, "do you really, truly think my plan will work?"

Sophia lifted her pen from the parchment and gazed at him. "We shall need to pray — pray very hard — that it does."

# CHAPTER 26

AFTER WAVING WHAT SHE'D WRITTEN IN THE AIR TO DRY, Sophia handed the parchment scrap to Fabrizio. "Give this to the Zeanzis and return as fast as you can with their reply. Remember, your plan — good as it is — depends on secrecy."

The rain was still coming down when Fabrizio burst out of the house. "With permission," he called to the soldiers across the way. "May I do a small errand for my household?"

"Our orders are only to keep people out," replied one of the soldiers.

Hiding the scrap of parchment in his tunic, Fabrizio ran off.

He reached Maria's house quickly. When he knocked on the door, Maria looked out, appearing much as she had when Fabrizio first saw her in the Hall of Justice — begrimed with ink. Seeing him, she grinned and pulled him into the main room.

"Fabrizio! Look! We've put the press back together."

The messy heap of odd pieces was gone, replaced by a large bulky table with six legs standing in the middle of the room. To Fabrizio's eyes it looked like a wine or olive press, but there were no grapes, no olives, nor the smell of either. Two middle legs rose up to the ceiling where they seemed to be attached and connected by a crossbeam, through which a long screw had been placed. Underneath the crossbeam was a long screw with a pole inserted sideways. At the bottom of the screw a flat piece hovered above the tabletop.

As Fabrizio looked on, Maria's father pushed the pole to the left, causing the screw to come down, which in turn caused its bottom flat piece to press onto a sheet of paper that lay atop the table.

Maria's mother bent over, closely observing the place where this flat piece pressed against the paper.

"Up!" she called. Maria's father pushed the pole in the opposite direction. The screw revolved, lifting the bottom plate from the table. As soon as it was high enough, Maria's mother stripped the paper away. Fabrizio could see that type — letter faceup — had been placed atop the table in something like a box.

Maria darted forward and, holding a great black ball of cloth, rubbed ink over the type. "Now you see what a printer's devil does," she told Fabrizio. "I just inked the type."

Her mother, meanwhile, held the paper in her two hands and studied it.

"Well?" asked Maria's father.

"It's working!" said her mother with great relief. She placed another piece of paper beneath the bottom plate, atop the type. Maria's father worked the rod; the screw went down and then up. The second piece of paper was drawn out.

"Mama," said Maria, "show them to Fabrizio."

The woman held out the two pieces of paper. Both contained a few words and they looked *exactly* the same.

"Forgive me. What does it say?" he asked.

Maria read what had been printed:

### The Zeanzi Printing Press is alive.

"It means that we're not dead, that we've put the press back together, and we can take it apart and go elsewhere."

"Where, hopefully, we will be appreciated," put in Signora Zeanzi.

Fabrizio made a bow. "Signore, Signora, I offer my deepest congratulations. And with my mistress's compliments," he said to Maria's father, "she wishes to know if you can . . . what you call . . . print something for her." He handed him the parchment.

Signor Zeanzi studied it and bowed to Fabrizio. "My dear boy, I'm truly grateful for the kindness you have shown Maria. But, by my life, I swore to your Count Scarazoni that we'd leave Pergamontio as soon as possible. And that we would not print anything else here."

"Signore, please, it's the only way to save my master."

"I don't know . . . the danger —"

"Papa," said Maria, "*you* made the promise to Count Scarazoni, not me. I can print it."

Signor Zeanzi looked at his wife.

"Without the boy's help we might not all be here," she said.

Signor Zeanzi nodded and handed Maria the scrap of parchment. "So be it."

Maria turned to Fabrizio. "How many do you need?"

"Enough for two hands."

"Easy enough. But you'll need to help."

"Thank you. I must tell my mistress."

Maria led him to the door. "The type will be set by the time you come back. We'll do the printing, then. And you can tell me about your plan."

"I'll return as fast as I can," said Fabrizio, and he sped home.

"Maria's parents were able to put their printing machine back together," he reported to Sophia. "I saw it working. It's amazing, Mistress. They made two pieces of writing, which, with my own eyes, I could see were exactly the same. It's truly magical."

"Excellent," said Sophia. "But will they do as we asked?"

"They won't, but Maria and I can. I'll need to go back and help her."

"Good. Now, while you were gone, I went and told the soldiers that the prince suggested you bring a coffin to the trial and requested permission. So that, too, is done."

"Mistress, forgive me, was it wise to tell anyone you've come home?"

Sophia blushed. "I didn't think of that. They were just soldiers. We'll hope for the best." She tried to smile.

There was a knock on the door.

"Keep out of sight," said Fabrizio and he ran to the door. One of the soldiers was standing there.

"Permission to visit the magician has been granted for this evening. A soldier will come for you this afternoon. Be ready."

"Who grants it?" asked Fabrizio.

"Prince Cosimo."

"Mistress," said Fabrizio when he returned to Sophia with the news, "we don't have much time. I still need to arrange for a donkey and cart. Then I must go to my friend and make those papers."

"I wish I could do more."

"Just stay completely hidden. In fact, best lock the door behind me."

Sophia gave him a hug and let him out the door. The rain had stopped. As Fabrizio leaped out onto the street, he heard Mistress Sophia bolt the door behind him. Feeling a sense of urgency, he ran as hard as he could.

# CHAPTER 27

ℑABRIZIO DASHED TO SIGNOR LOTI'S OLIVE OIL STORE around the corner. The old man was working on his oil press with two of his apprentices.

"Signore," said Fabrizio, "I have no time to explain, but my master and mistress are in great distress and beg permission to borrow your cart and donkey this afternoon and evening."

"I'm sorry to hear such news," said Signor Loti, not for a moment ceasing to work the press. "But, of course, they may borrow it."

"A million thanks, Signore," cried Fabrizio. "I shall be back." He tore away.

"I've been wondering where you were," said Maria as she drew him into her house. "I have everything ready."

Fabrizio looked around. "Where are your parents?"

"They don't want to have anything to do with this job. So they went out. We have to do this alone."

Fabrizio bowed. "Signorina Devil," he said, "you need only tell me what to do."

"I've set the type," Maria explained. "And locked it in with the wedges."

She handed Fabrizio an inky black ball of wool. "I need to keep my hands clean. So this time you're the printer's devil. There's the ink." She pointed to a wooden box in which cloth was stuffed. The cloth was black with ink. "Dip your pad in that ink and rub it over the letters. Do it as evenly as possible."

"Like this?" Fabrizio asked.

"Not too much ink, nor too little."

They set to work. Maria stripped away the first paper, looked at it, and held it up for Fabrizio to see.

"Forgive me," he said, "I can't read it very well."

She laughed. "A printer's devil has to read."

Within the hour some fifty papers were printed. They spread them about the room to dry. Once dried they made a bundle, which Maria tied together with string. As they worked, Fabrizio told her about his plan.

"And do you really think it will work?"

"We have no choice."

"When will you leave for the trial?" she asked.

"This afternoon." Holding the papers in his arms, he went to the door and was just about to open it, when he halted.

"What's the matter?" said Maria.

Fabrizio put his finger to his lips. "I heard a voice right outside." He opened the window shutter a small gap, peeked out, and jumped back.

"What is it?"

"There's a troop of blue coats out front." He ran through the house to the back room and spied out. "No one." He pulled open the door. "I'm going."

"I'm going with you," said Maria. "To make sure you're safe."

"What about your parents?"

"I'll tell them later."

"Maria . . ."

"Go!"

They jumped into the alley. Even as they did, a troop of blue coats appeared at the far end.

"Run!" cried Fabrizio, and he tore down the alley in the opposite direction. Maria was right at his heels. Only when Fabrizio was sure they were safe did he stop.

"What does it mean?" asked Maria.

"I don't know. But I must make sure Mistress is safe."

Running, Fabrizio took as roundabout a way as he knew. At every corner he checked for signs of soldiers. They saw many.

"Are they looking for you?" asked Maria.

"I hope not."

They ran on and didn't stop until they reached the Street of the Olive Merchants. When they arrived, Fabrizio stole a look around the corner.

A carriage stood in front of the house.

"Maria!"

She looked and saw what Fabrizio had seen: blue coats milling about Mangus's door. The door had been broken.

The next moment Mistress Sophia was escorted out of the house and pushed into the carriage. It was a matter of moments until it lumbered away, the soldiers running after it.

# CHAPTER 28

Maria and Fabrizio rushed to the house and stood gazing helplessly in the direction in which the carriage had gone.

"I'm sure it was the prince who took her," said Fabrizio. "Mistress should never have talked to the soldiers."

They pushed the bashed-in door back into place as best they could, then stepped into the hallway. "It feels deserted," said Fabrizio.

He led the way into the study, where they sat down. It was a long while before Fabrizio could speak again. When he did he said, "Cosimo will do anything to make certain Scarazoni is accused. You'll see, he'll be sure Master knows he has Mistress Sophia so he can make Master say it was Scarazoni who tried to topple the king."

"Would your master do that?"

Fabrizio shrugged. "For Mistress's sake he would. I would, too."

"Then your whole plan is . . . gone."

Fabrizio didn't reply. He placed the bundle of papers they had printed on the table, and stared at it.

"Fabrizio . . ." Maria said after a while.

Fabrizio could not even look at her.

"I'll take your mistress's place. In the coffin."

Fabrizio lifted his eyes. "You will?"

She nodded.

"It will be very dangerous."

"I'm still willing."

"W . . . why?"

"Look how awful your prince is. A murderer. He did all this to your master. And mistress. He tried to execute you. He destroyed our printing press. With DeLaBina, he had me arrested. Even if my parents and I go free, we'll have to move. I want to do *something.*"

"You'd have to lie in the coffin a long time. A really long time. And . . . there's nothing sure about what will happen."

Maria nodded again. "I still want to do it."

"You're not a devil. You're an angel." Fabrizio stood up. "Come. I'll show you the coffin."

* * *

After showing Maria the coffin and explaining about the false bottom, Fabrizio went out and returned with Signor Loti's old gray donkey and his two-wheeled cart. He left it in the narrow alley behind the house. A load of hay was provided for the donkey, who was content to stand patiently, nibbling on his food.

In the alley, with no one watching, Fabrizio and Maria hauled the coffin from the house and set it onto the cart. It was heavy and bulky. Once it almost fell. But they managed to get it loaded and tied down. Fabrizio even placed a blanket inside for Maria's comfort.

"We have to make sure you look like a ghost," said Fabrizio.

They searched Mistress Sophia's bedroom and found white powder, along with a white shift. Maria daubed her face, arms, and neck, even her red hair.

With everything ready, Fabrizio and Maria waited in the hallway for the soldiers to summon them.

"Fabrizio," Maria said suddenly. "You've never told me when I'm supposed to show myself."

"Mistress and I only agreed that she would listen to what was happening. She was going to decide for herself."

Maria said nothing, but Fabrizio could see she was more nervous than before. "A million, million thanks for your courage," he said.

Fabrizio kept looking outside, waiting for soldiers to come. Rapidly churning storm clouds had turned the sky dark. A cold wind rattled shutters and swirled the street dust. A clay pot was dislodged from some ledge and fell, smashing. Thunder rumbled. Fabrizio felt tense.

Finally, a knock sounded on the door.

Fabrizio jumped up and opened it. A soldier stood waiting.

"Signore," said Fabrizio, "Prince Cosimo directed me to bring a coffin. My donkey and cart are out back."

"Lead it around. Hurry."

Fabrizio rushed into the study and grabbed the papers. He and Maria dashed through the courtyard and out into the alley. They opened the coffin lid. Maria climbed in and lay down. Fabrizio placed the papers on her chest.

"Ready?"

"I hope so."

"God keep you safe," Fabrizio whispered, then he set the false bottom over her. A few pounds of his fist and it snapped in.

It was late afternoon when they set off, the sun lost in the lowering skies. Fabrizio led the donkey by a short, frayed rope. The plodding, long-eared beast made no protest, no sound, and very little speed. The two-wheeled cart trundled along with considerable clatter. The coffin, though tied down, bounced. Ahead of them, a soldier, carrying a sword, marched.

The air had grown cold, with occasional winds slapping down in short wet bursts. It made the stone-paved road they were following slippery, leading as it did steeply uphill. The road was twisty, too, now and again doubling back, winding its narrow way between closely clustered houses. Fortunately, the donkey proved sure-footed.

The few people out on the streets paused respectfully when they saw the coffin roll by. Fabrizio had no trouble looking solemn. He felt it. He grew even more so when black birds, high in the darkening sky, wheeled and called raucously, making him wonder if they were giving him a warning.

He glanced back at the donkey cart, hoping that Maria was comfortable. For his own part, he brooded over the things that might go wrong. So many! Would they be able to free Master? What had happened to Mistress? Would Maria suffer? Would he?

Now and again he stole looks at the summit, where the vast Castello was perched. With every step they took it seemed to grow larger and more menacing. He was already chilled. To see the fortifications loom so made him feel colder, tenser. The Castello seemed to be so full of power and he so powerless. *I think that's why I love magic,* he told himself. *It gives secret powers.*

By the time they reached the Castello's outer walls, twilight had come. The great gray stones and darkening skies seemed to meld. The wind had picked up. Rain showers spit down out of the churning mists with increasing frequency and force. Everything seemed soaked in damp, gray rot.

They skirted the fortification walls and reached the place they had come the night before. With shoulders scrunched, cold rain trickling down his neck, puddles gathering around his feet, Fabrizio peered around. He could see now: The crypt was adjacent to, though not quite part of, the Castello.

The lead soldier guided them to the door Fabrizio had used the night before. A few shivering soldiers stood on guard. The door was unlocked. Fabrizio was ordered to enter.

"With permission, Signore," said Fabrizio, "I'll need help with the coffin."

"Who is it for?"

"My master is on trial, and alas, it may be for him."

"Ah! Mangus the Magician!"

"Yes, Signore."

"You're right," said the soldier. "He'll need it."

"Wait!" said another. "We've been ordered to check everything that goes in." He approached the coffin and lifted the lid.

Fabrizio, heart pounding, watched.

The soldier looked in. "Nothing," he announced and dropped the lid.

Three of the soldiers gripped the coffin handles. Fabrizio grasped another. Like pallbearers, they marched through the entryway.

The door slammed behind them.

# CHAPTER 29

ONLY A FLICKERING LIGHT AT THE END OF THE TUNNEL showed them the way. As they walked the fifty yards, no one spoke. The sound of the storm gradually faded, replaced by the rasping scrape of their shoes on rough ground.

They stepped into the room with the domed ceiling. Count Scarazoni was there holding a flaming torch. Fabrizio noticed that on his belt, within easy reach, was his long, pointed dagger.

"My lord," whispered Fabrizio, making a slight bow.

"Why have you brought a coffin?" the count demanded.

"The prince suggested it."

Scarazoni frowned. "Did you tell Mangus what he must do?"

"Yes, my lord."

The count approached the coffin, lifted the lid, and looked in. Next moment he let the lid drop, turned, and said, "Follow me."

The soldiers and Fabrizio carried the coffin into the ancient crypt. The room was cold and damp. It smelled of decay. Though he had seen them before, Fabrizio could not keep his eyes from the great piles of bones and skulls set against the crumbling walls. *God keep us from being part of these piles,* he prayed.

A high-backed chair, flanked on either side by two benches, had been brought into the room. There were two standing candelabra whose fluttering candlelight seemed to make the room's stone walls tremble.

"With permission," said Fabrizio, "where shall I put the coffin?"

"Out of the way," said Scarazoni.

Fabrizio looked around and noticed a shadowy place next to one of the entrances. He guided the soldiers to it. The coffin was set down. He stood nearby.

"Very well," said Scarazoni. "I'll fetch the king and the others."

"With permission, what others?"

"The royal family." The count turned away.

"My lord!"

Scarazoni stopped and looked back.

"I should tell you that the prince had his soldiers come to my master's house and take my mistress away."

"When?"

"Earlier today."

"To threaten Mangus," said the count.

"I think so," said Fabrizio.

Scarazoni stood still, frowning. For the first time Fabrizio saw uncertainty in his face. "The king is waiting. It's too late to change things."

Fabrizio watched Scarazoni walk out of the room. He touched the coffin and whispered, "God grant us success." Moments later, Scarazoni reappeared with twelve helmeted green-coated soldiers. Each was armed with swords that gleamed in the candlelight. At Scarazoni's command, they arrayed themselves in a row behind the central chair.

Next to enter the crypt was King Claudio, dressed entirely in black. He paled as he gazed upon the heaps of bones. And when he noticed the coffin, Fabrizio saw his jaw clench and his hands tighten into fists.

To Fabrizio's dismay, the king drew close. He motioned to a soldier to open the coffin lid. The soldier darted forward and lifted it. Claudio leaned over and peered in.

Fabrizio was afraid to look.

Apparently satisfied with what he saw, the king turned and made his way to the makeshift throne. He sat uneasily, as if unable to find comfort.

The two princes, first Cosimo and then the younger prince, Lorenzo, entered. Both were dressed elegantly, in feather hats, jackets, capes, and colored boots. The moment Lorenzo saw the crypt's contents his smile faded. He glanced at the king and at Count Scarazoni, who returned his look with a scowl of contempt.

As for Cosimo, he made a curt, mocking bow, after which the prince and his brother sat on one of the benches to the left of the king.

Next to come was a woman whom Fabrizio recognized as Queen Jovanna. She was thin, with a small, intense, oval face. With the queen was a veiled girl. Fabrizio supposed it was the princess Teresina, the youngest of the royal children. They, too, halted and, wide-eyed, looked about the crypt before sitting down on a bench to the right of the king.

Next to come, guided by a soldier, was Agrippa. The executioner looked everywhere, clearly fascinated by all he saw. When he noticed Fabrizio, his face lit up with a broad smile. He took a step in the boy's direction, only to be restrained by a soldier and led into a far corner where he was told to remain.

His appearance appalled Fabrizio. It suggested what most likely would happen.

Once the royals were seated, there was much shifting and anxious adjusting of legs, hands, and arms. No one spoke. Fabrizio felt the tension in the room tighten.

Two blue-coated soldiers marched in. Between them was Mistress Sophia. When she looked around, a hand went to her mouth. Even in the gloom of the room, Fabrizio could see how alarmed she was. She lifted a hand as if to reach for Fabrizio, only to be restrained by one of her guards.

Then Fabrizio saw her notice the coffin. She turned to gaze at him. He was afraid to offer more than a darting look.

But Cosimo must have noticed. He stood suddenly and sauntered over to the coffin. He lifted the lid and peered inside only to let the lid drop with a crash. The sound echoed through the chamber.

Without looking at Fabrizio, but in a low voice, Cosimo said, "Let's hope we do not have to fill it."

"Proceed!" cried the king.

"Bring in the prisoner," called Scarazoni.

Four more blue-coated soldiers escorted Mangus into the room. The old man walked slowly, head bowed. His clothing was torn and dirty. To Fabrizio's eyes, he seemed exhausted.

He was led to the center of the room and made to stand before the king and the other royals. They gazed at him, eyes full of dread and fascination. The king, in particular, seemed uncomfortable. He continually shifted around, hands in motion, as if one hand were washing the other.

Prince Cosimo, gazing at Mangus, lost his jaunty manner. He wiggled about in his chair but continued to watch the magician through lidded eyes, even as he touched his mustache.

*They truly fear him,* thought Fabrizio.

Mangus looked around. When he saw Mistress Sophia, he cried out and made a step toward her only to be held back by the soldiers.

The old man ceased to struggle but continued to look at his wife. Fabrizio saw her eyes shift. Mangus followed her gaze to the coffin.

Prince Cosimo, watching Mangus, smiled weakly.

Facing the king, Mangus, his hands clasped, stood a little straighter, creating the appearance of composure. All the same, though it was very cold in the crypt, Fabrizio was sure he saw small beads of sweat on the old man's brow.

Count Scarazoni stepped forward. "Majesties, we are here to conduct the trial of your subject Mangus — for treason. Let us begin."

# CHAPTER 30

𝔚E ALL . . . KNOW WHY . . . WE ARE HERE," SAID THE king, his fingers thrumming nervously on his knees so that his rings clicked and clacked one against the other. He pointed at Mangus. "That man is a . . . a magician! Magic is forbidden in Pergamontio!"

Mangus made a dignified bow, his face calm.

The count stepped forward. "Indeed, Majesty, magic may or may not be a factor here. What we do know is that the Primo Magistrato Brutus DeLaBina — who was murdered — provided a license for a diabolical machine capable of making many papers calling for your removal."

"Nonsense," cried the king. "No machine could do such magic. It was Mangus! With magic. He was plotting with DeLaBina and someone else."

"Yes, Majesty. But that *someone*" — he darted a cold look at Fabrizio — "killed DeLaBina to keep him from confessing the conspiracy and implicating him. We are here to discover the guilty party."

240

Hearing the count's words, Fabrizio felt a stab of unease. Perhaps he was wrong to have believed Scarazoni was going to help Master. Perhaps he *was* the principal tormentor.

Even as he had the thought, Prince Cosimo leaned toward his father and whispered into his ear.

The king nodded and called out, "I don't care about DeLaBina. He's dead. This trial is about Mangus and his magic. I intend to find out who ordered him to make those papers! You, Count, seem to have known about him but did nothing to stop his magic. Stand aside! *I* will conduct this trial."

Fabrizio saw Scarazoni's brows contract. His face flushed with fury, he opened his mouth, but it took a few moments for him to speak.

"Majesty," said Scarazoni, "I believe —"

"Did you not hear me?" the king's voice boomed. "Stand aside!"

A smile played upon Prince Cosimo's lips.

Fabrizio saw Scarazoni's hand move toward his dagger.

Then he moved off to one side, posting himself near one of the entryways.

"You!" cried the king, pointing right at Mangus. "Will you confess to being a magician?"

"Majesty," returned the old man, "I confess only to offering the *illusion* of magic."

Fabrizio saw the king glance at Prince Cosimo, as if seeking his approval or advice.

The prince gave a small nod.

The king shifted and again addressed Mangus. "Illusion or not, it's still *magic*. Magic is not just evil. It's illegal in Pergamontio. Those who practice magic must be punished by death. I ask you, Magician, who else besides DeLaBina did you conspire with to produce those papers?"

"I did not conspire with anyone, Your Majesty."

The king shifted awkwardly in his chair. Fabrizio wondered if he was saying practiced words or finding his way.

Prince Cosimo whispered into his ear again.

The king nodded. "A few nights ago, you," he said, "in my city, performed magic before a mob. While doing so, you snatched images of me from the air. And then made me disappear! Is that true?"

"I confess to creating an illusion, Your Majesty."

"Did you tell the crowd it was an illusion?" Prince Cosimo called out.

Mangus wavered. "I confess that I did not, my lord."

"What *did* you tell them?" the prince demanded.

Mangus thought hard.

"Answer him!" insisted the king.

Before Mangus could reply, the prince shouted, "You said, 'For my final act of magic, I shall create something from nothing. Furthermore, from that something, I shall make . . . many!'"

"How do you know he said that?" demanded the count.

The prince stood up. "Bring in the witnesses!"

As if waiting for the command, more soldiers entered the room. With them came Benito and Giuseppe.

The two entered with a swagger, but the moment they saw Mangus and Mistress Sophia, they hesitated and averted their eyes.

"Signori," said the prince to them, "as servants to this magician, you were at that performance. Did not the magician say 'For my final act of magic, I shall create something from nothing'? 'Furthermore, from that something, I shall make . . . many!'"

"My lord," said Benito, bowing and bobbing, "it was only —"

"Yes or no!" cried the prince.

"Yes, my lord," whispered Benito.

"Enough," said the prince. "Put them back in their cell!"

"But" — Giuseppe tried to speak — "you said . . ."

Though the two protested, they were led away.

The king sat up and leaned forward. "Magician!" he shouted. "I command you — on pain of the most severe punishment, death — to use your magic to reveal who it was that ordered the making of those papers."

"Majesty," said the old man in an even voice, "you command me to use magic to reveal the truth. But you have just informed me that those who do magic shall be punished. If I refuse to act as you ask, I'll be punished.

If I act as you wish, I will still be punished. What am I to do?"

The king passed a hand over his face, rubbed his eyes, and pulled at his beard. Everyone was staring at him.

"Very well," he said, petulantly beating a fist on his knee. "Mangus, we promise that no bodily harm shall come to you if you do your magic. But this holds true *only* if your magic reveals the one who ordered the papers. Now do so!"

Mangus stood perfectly still, his eyes closed. Fabrizio, watching him, kept thinking, *Now is the time to use your magic!*

The room grew silent. Every eye stared at Mangus.

The king sighed audibly. His body tensed. "Mangus," he yelled, "use your magic!"

From within the coffin a banging began.

Fabrizio jumped. The others, equally taken aback, swung around and stared. So, too, did Mangus. The soldiers gripped their swords. The queen put her hand to her throat. Her younger children sat up stiffly. Scarazoni came forward a few steps.

245

Mangus recovered quickly. He stood straight, arms spread wide, fingers extended in clawlike fashion.

"Hovering spirits of darkness," he cried, "Mangus the Magician calls upon you! Rise up from the depths of your death! You, who are dead, reveal the murderer of DeLaBina. Reveal the one who conspired against the king. Come back to the living that the living might know about death! Come! Return! Reveal the traitor!"

More banging.

Fabrizio's scalp tightened. The hairs on the back of his neck stood up. He wanted to swallow. It was impossible.

The king was now sitting at the very edge of his chair, one hand touching his mouth, the other hand open before him, fingers spread wide, as if to defend himself.

The queen was staring, too. Prince Cosimo's mouth was agape, his body pitched forward. Count Scarazoni leaned in, his hand resting on his dagger.

"Come, specters of darkness," exclaimed Mangus. "In the name of truth, now is the time to rise up!"

The banging continued. Fabrizio grasped what was

happening: Maria was trying to push up the false bottom. It had stuck.

Next moment, the coffin lid burst open, smashing against the wall with a great *smack* that reverberated throughout the crypt.

Then, Maria sat up inside the coffin.

The king gasped and leaped to his feet.

In the dimness, Maria's face was so uniformly white as to appear almost featureless. By contrast, her white-powdered body seemed to glow. Strands of her red hair poked through the powder and looked like dripping blood. As if writhing in torment, she waved her ghostly pale arms.

"Spirit of death!" cried Mangus. "Bring us the truth. Tell us who committed these great crimes!"

Fabrizio watched as Maria stood up and stepped out of the coffin. The papers were in her hand. Momentarily, she seemed at a loss for which way to go, turning in different directions. Then, fastening on the king, she advanced toward him.

The king gasped, dropped into his chair, and pushed himself back as far as he could go.

Maria drew closer to him. The room was stone silent. Everyone stared at the ghostly figure. With a sudden motion, Maria flung the papers out and up. They scattered through the air and settled on all the royals.

After a moment of hesitation, they grabbed them and read them.

### Prince Cosimo — Traitor and Murderer!

The king, eyes wide, mouth open, stared with astonishment at the first paper he had snatched. He looked at another. And another. The others did the same.

Prince Cosimo stood, one of the papers clutched in his hand. "Stop! In God's name. Stop!" He spun around and threw himself down at the king's feet. "Father. Forgive me! I killed DeLaBina. I conspired against you! Forgive me! I confess!"

"The light!" screamed the king. "Bring the light!"

Count Scarazoni rushed forward and lit the candles.

Prince Cosimo jumped to his feet. It seemed as if he were about to leap upon the king.

Claudio sat back in his chair, staring at his son with a look of horror. So, too, were the queen and the junior royals. Even Mangus and Sophia looked on, astonished.

Next moment, the prince wheeled around and ran toward one of the entryways. Fabrizio, standing by, stepped in front of him, lunged, and grabbed him around the waist.

"Let me go!" cried the prince. "Let me go!"

Though dragged along, Fabrizio held on long enough for soldiers to run forward and grab the prince and hold him.

"Bring him here!" cried the king.

The soldiers hauled the prince back to his father. As they did, Fabrizio looked about and realized that, in the confusion, Maria had vanished. He spun around just in time to catch sight of her racing down the tunnel, away from the crypt, toward the outer wall.

"Fool! Betrayer!" the king shouted at Cosimo, who was standing before him, held by the soldiers. "Murderer! You are my son. I shall not hang you. But you are herewith banished from Pergamontio. In exile, *forever*. I proclaim your brother, Prince Lorenzo, to be the heir to my rule! Lead him away."

Count Scarazoni made a hand motion to the soldiers, who came forward and marched the weeping Prince Cosimo out of the room. Scarazoni started after them, only to pause at the entryway. He turned and sought out Fabrizio with his eyes. "Boy!" he hissed.

Fabrizio spun around.

"Well done," he said. Then he turned to the king. "Majesty!" he called out. "Remember your promise to the magician. Show mercy!" Then he turned and followed the soldiers out.

Fabrizio stared after him. *Master is saved!*

The queen took her other children by the hand and rushed out of the room.

The only ones left were the king, Mangus, Mistress Sophia, and Fabrizio. And Agrippa.

No one spoke. The king remained slumped in his chair.

"Magician," said the king, breathing heavily, his voice full of agony. "You have done what I have asked you to do.

I pronounce you guilty of doing magic. But — Count Scarazoni has reminded me of my promise. You shall live. All the same, you are herewith forbidden the practice of magic of *any* kind. Henceforward you are confined to your home for as long as I wish. No one may visit you. I never want to see or hear of you again."

With that, King Claudio rose up and staggered out of the crypt.

No sooner did he leave than Agrippa came forward.

"Fabrizio!" he cried. "What wonderful magic!" He lumbered over, grabbed the boy's hand, and shook it. "Bringing the dead back alive. That's exactly the kind of magic I could make use of. Kill them, restore them. The best trick ever. Signore, you must come back and teach me how to do it. I honor you." He bowed and lumbered out of the crypt.

Sophia, meanwhile, had gone to Mangus. The two embraced. Only then did a smiling Mangus turn to Fabrizio. "Fabrizio! I was praying you would do something like that. How did you manage it?"

Fabrizio grinned. "With permission, Master," he said with a bow. "Everything surprises if we lack knowledge of it."

# CHAPTER 31

TAKING ONE OF THE CANDLES TO LIGHT THEIR WAY, Fabrizio guided Mangus and Sophia back through the tunnel.

"Fabrizio," whispered Mistress Sophia, "that person in the coffin. Who was it?"

"My friend Maria. You need to meet her."

"And I need to thank her for her help and bravery," said Mangus.

Maria was waiting by the outer door, wiping the white powder from her face. "Did I do it right?" she asked, grinning.

"Perfect!" Fabrizio cried. "Master, Mistress, with permission, my good friend Maria, the printer's devil."

Both Mangus and Sophia bowed. "We thank you," they said together.

When they stepped outside, Scarazoni's carriage was waiting. Mangus and Sophia sat on one side, Fabrizio and Maria on the other.

As they moved down the hill toward the city, Mangus leaned forward and grasped Fabrizio's hand.

"Fabrizio," he said, his voice soft. "Do you . . . do you recall when I was in the prison cell and I, unthankful sinner, released you from my service?"

"Master . . ."

"I beg you to forgive me," said Mangus. "I fear I've been too harsh. You have served me well. More than well. Be assured, Fabrizio, I want you to stay. And you will stay, won't you?"

"With permission, Master, yes. And yes again."

The cathedral bells began to toll. It was midnight.

Next morning, Fabrizio went to say his good-byes to Maria. The Zeanzis' printing press had been taken apart and loaded into a cart with their possessions. She and her family were about to leave for Naples.

"I have a farewell gift for you," said Maria, and into the palm of his right hand, she dropped a small pile of metal type. "It's the letters of your name," she explained.

"If you ever write a book, you'll have to start with the printing. And I promise to supply the other letters."

"I think," said Fabrizio, "before I write a book, I first need to learn to read."

"Hold out your other hand," said Maria.

When Fabrizio did, Maria took the pieces of type and set them in proper order.

Fabrizio studied them intently. "F-A-B-R-I-Z-I-O," he said, calling out one letter at a time. Then with a grin, he said, "Fabrizio!"